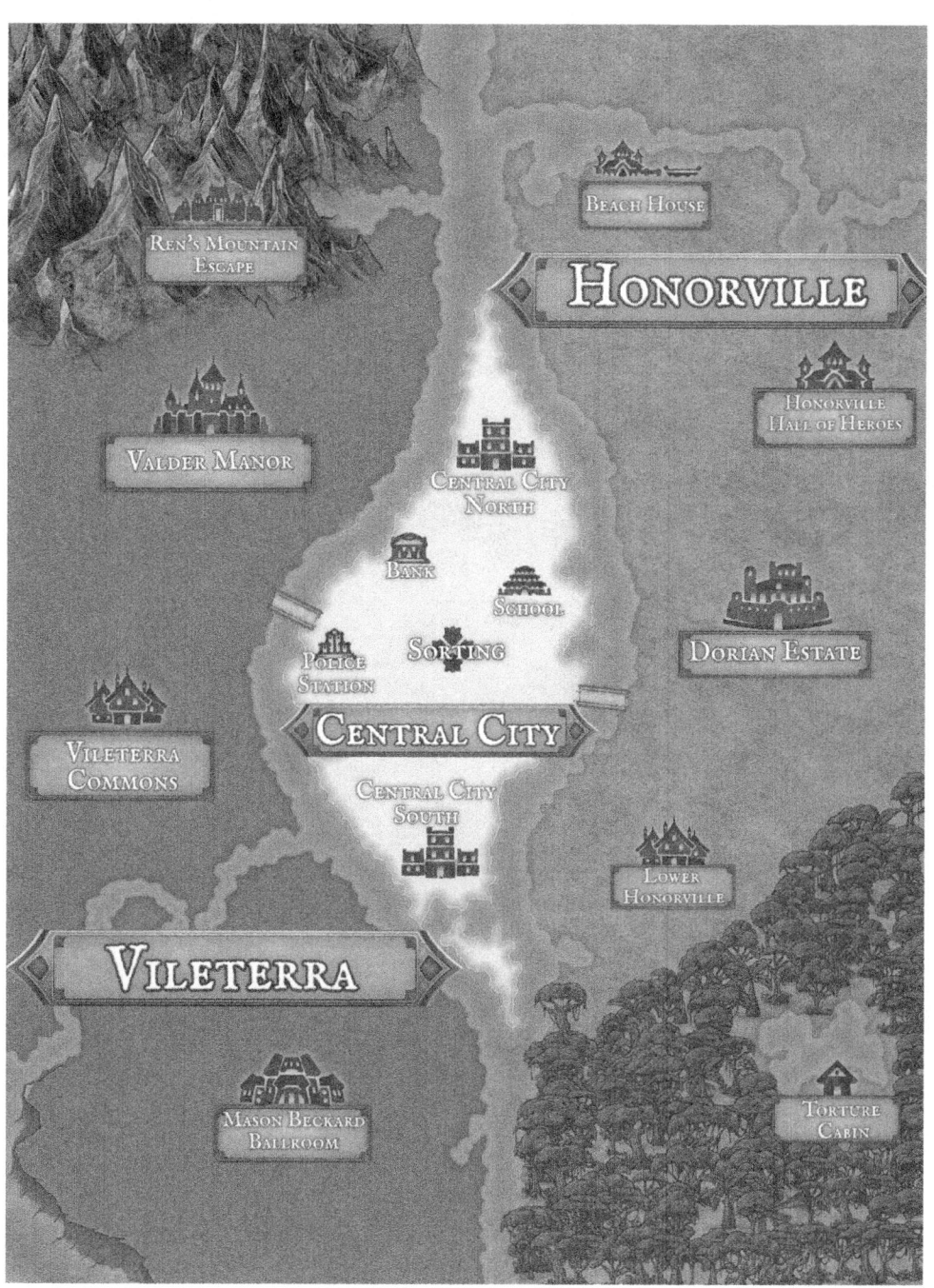

Caution: This book contains scenes of violence, death, nudity, sex, weapons, drinking, crude language, detailed torture, severe mental trauma, abuse, PTSD, stalking, starvation, drugging others without their knowledge, and gore. Do not read if you are uncomfortable with any such topics.

Copyright © 2022 Anna Lynn Hammar

All rights reserved. No part of this book may be reproduced or used in any manner without the prior written permission of the copyright owner, except for the use of brief quotations in book reviews. To request permissions, contact the author at: AuthorAnnaLynnHammar@gmail.com

Hardcover: 9798846138087
Paperback: 9798841257028
 First Paperback Edition: October 2022

MORALLY GRAY

Anna Lynn Hammar

"I love you as certain dark things are to be loved, in secret, between the shadow and the soul."
– Pablo Neruda

Prologue

Jinx stood with her hands wringing in front of her. Two years before, her brother was in this same position, possibly equally as nervous as she was now. Everything turned out fine for him, everything would be fine for her too.

"Don't slouch, Jinx," Her mother fret, tugging on the bow that refused to stay straight on her back.

Jinx stood straighter, lifting her chin to appear confident. She didn't want to look bad when she was announced, especially if she was sorted as a Love Interest.

Her mother had spent hours perfecting her hair and makeup, spending more money to have a custom dress made just for her. She was excited for her sorting, happy with whatever option given to her so long as she wasn't a Background Character.

In her school classes she learned about the six options for the sorting. Hero, Love Interest, Best Friend, Villain, Henchman, and Background Character. Her mother and father were a Hero-Love Interest match, her brother sorted into Hero after his school graduation. Now, it was her turn.

"Don't fuss too much, Liv, she looks wonderful." Her dad said, smiling down at her.

Olivia looked down at her daughter with a wary smile, her red painted lips never once smearing onto her pristine white teeth. Her blonde hair was laid in waves over her shoulders and down her back, a golden barrette holding back her bangs. She wore a slim, red dress with a golden belt over her waist, matching Jinx's father's tie. There was always a red tinted aura around her mother, one Jinx had realized early in childhood, no one else saw.

Her father wore a tan suit with a brown undershirt. His golden tie the only pop of color. His blond hair had replicated onto her brother, along with his golden skin.

Both of her parents looked at her with pride sparkling in their eyes, but her mother did still look worried.

"Jinx Dorian, you're next." A stagehand called out to her.

Jinx looked to the stagehand and then her parents, nerves fluttering loose inside her stomach.

Her mother kissed her cheek, her father turning her towards the stage as they walked back to the crowd to watch.

Jinx walked closer to the entrance, looking out at the kid who went before her.

He was in many of her classes, but they never talked. He was tall with dark black hair and pale skin. He had sharp green eyes that were always narrowed as if he had been judging everything he saw. His parents were Villains, a strange combination since it was typical that a Villain and Henchmen made a pair. Though, she knew him better than most of her classmates. His father being the arch nemesis for hers.

"Ren Valder. Age: eighteen." The electronic voice announced. "Sorting."

There was silence as the lights around the auditorium dimmed and only a single blue spotlight showed onto Ren. Jinx's heart beat in her chest as she realized she would be standing in that spotlight next.

Ren's head moved, their eyes catching. He looked her up and down, then smirked, turning his attention back to the crowd. Jinx felt her heart drop, looking down at her outfit to see if something was wrong.

The light changed colors to a deep red over Ren, the announcer's voice coming soon after. "Villain. Hero pair: Micha Torrance."

Ren walked off the stage, greeted by his father who patted him happily on the back.

"It's your turn Ms. Dorian." The stagehand said.

Jinx nodded, blowing out a loud breath and walked forward. She forced her back straight, her chin high, placing one foot in front of the other. She found her place in the middle of the stage, turning to face the crowd.

"Jinx Dorian. Age: eighteen. Sorting." The voice said.

Jinx tried to hold her hands at her side, praying for a good sort. She had a plan and she needed anything but a-.

"Background Character."

The blue light that had focused on her went gray. Her whole body froze, the smile that was on her face had dropped. She looked to her parents, but they did not look to her. This wasn't good, she couldn't disgrace her family like this. What would happen when she got home? What would she expect from this public humiliation?

"Get off the stage." The stagehand ordered, waving at her.

She opened and closed her mouth, her head looking down in shame. Jinx caught her feet over the floor, tripping and stumbling so that she landed on the stage in a crawling position.

A hand encircled her arm, warmth coming to her body from it.

She looked up, seeing the blond hair and soft smile of her brother, Thaddeus. "Come on, Jinny."

Tears clouded her vision as she allowed her brother to help her off the stage. The announcer's voice continued behind her, along with the flashing lights, but Jinx couldn't focus on the others.

"Serves those Dorians right to have a BC daughter," A kid sorted into Henchman said to the side. "We don't need another Dorian good guy."

The other kids gave a chorus of their agreements, Jinx wishing she could just hide within herself. All she needed was anything besides a Background Character. Now, her life goal was ruined.

"Don't listen to them," Thaddeus said strained, "You will be a wonderful Hero, I will make sure of it."

Jinx shook her head. "I was sorted Thad, I will only ever be a Background Character."

Thaddeus didn't object to her statement, causing Jinx to feel worse. Even if it was a lie, she wanted him to tell her it was okay.

She didn't remember much of the night after, only looking out the window of their car as they drove back to Honorville. Her dreams were ruined that day, she would never have the chance to fulfill the destiny she had carved for herself. The one she had desperately wanted to achieve.

Jinx would live a boring and unsensational life.

Chapter One
The Incident

Jinx Dorian sat at a metal table with her sweaty hands clasped onto each other. There was no other light in the room besides the single bulb that hung from a spot right above her head. The floor beneath her was smoothed rock, the walls matching it, only a bit more jagged. A single door was carved into a spot on her left, and while wooden, she was convinced it once was a jail cell.

She had never been in trouble before. She was not genetically predisposed to it according to the sorting. However, when her brother had told her he was leaving on a quest, everything had changed.

The wooden door to her left opened with a thud, causing Jinx to jump. She looked up to see the commissioner. The bags under his eyes were dark, accentuated by wrinkles. She could not see the lively brown color that he once had, only the darkness of a man who has seen too much. His once blond hair was thinning, more gray present than in his pictures on the billboards. His button-down shirt was wrinkled, a coffee stain present over his right pec.

"Ms. Dorian, was it?" He asked in a grumble.

"Yes, sir." She said.

"Any relation to Olivia and Packard Dorian?"

"My parents, sir."

He took a rough seat, slapping a folder onto the table as he looked to her. The stubble on his cheeks was amplified by the single light above them, causing his features to contort into a more intimidating appearance.

"I didn't know Olivia and Packard had a daughter, I only knew of your brother, Thaddeus." He stated, flipping open the folder. A picture of her identification was paperclipped inside, along with a copy of her sorting card. "Oh, you were sorted into BC."

Jinx hated the nickname for her sort. She was not BC; she was a Background Character.

"Yes sir." She sighed waiting for the comments she knew was coming next.

"It must've been disappointing for your parents to find out since they were a Hero and Love Interest. But at least your brother was sorted into Hero."

Jinx didn't react to the unintended insult anymore. She had heard it from everyone, including her own family.

"But we are not here to discuss your original sort, are we?" He asked hypothetically, "Tell me what happened from the point of Thaddeus' disappearance."

Jinx nodded, twirling her thumbs. "It had started when Thad had asked to come over…"

The phone ringing had woken Jinx up. She rolled over in her queen bed, fiddling with the thing to pick it up.

"Hello?" She asked in a groggy voice.

"Jinx, its me." Thad's voice said on the other side.

"Thaddeus?"

"Yes, your brother, hey can I come over?" He asked, there was a happiness to his tone.

Jinx rolled over, looking to the clock that read four in the morning. "This can't wait until at least seven?"

"No, I'll be gone by then." He said.

Jinx sighed, her head falling back onto her pillow. "Sure, Thad, come on over."

"Glad you agree, I'm outside your door." He chuckled.

Jinx hung up the phone without saying goodbye, slipping on her flipflops that she left beside her bed and shuffled to the door. She managed to braid her long brown hair before reaching the handle, opening it to see her grinning brother on her apartment porch.

Even with it being four in the morning, Thaddeus looked good. His blond hair was swept perfectly to the side, his teeth whitened and straight in his smile. His clothes were unusual though, especially with the bag he had slung over his shoulder filled with camping equipment.

She moved, letting Thad inside, then closed the door.

"What is all of this?" Jinx asked, walking to the kitchen to make a pot of coffee.

"I'm going on a quest." He said proudly.

Jinx nodded, patting away a yawn. "For what?"

"So, there's this dial, right? It can change the world as we know it! Whoever touches it will be able to change things for the better or worse with just a thought." He exclaimed, practically bouncing on her couch.

Jinx set down a cup of coffee in front of him, made with hazelnut creamer, his favorite.

"Isn't that dangerous though?" She asked sitting into her favorite chair. "What if you think something bad when you touch it, then the world could become fucked accidentally."

Thad shook his head. "I know it seems risky to you, since you're only a Background Character, but I'm a Hero, Jinx, I know what I'm doing."

Jinx looked into her cup at the swirling tan liquid. She was born into a roll of no significance, the sorting ceremony ruining her hopes and dreams.

"When are you leaving?" She asked without emotion.

Thad looked at his watch, quickly setting down his cup and going towards the door. "Now if I'm going to make it!"

"Make it? Thad, where do you have to go?" Jinx asked, quickly following him as he made his way out the door.

"I'll be back soon, Jinx, and when I'm back, everything will change!" He called to her.

Jinx watched as her brother walked down the streets of Central City South, sipping from her coffee cup. She waited long after he had disappeared to return inside to get ready for work.

After showering, she blew out her hair, throwing it up into a voluminous bun on the top of her head. She lined her eyes with a classy amount of eyeliner and mascara, a tint of lip gloss to liven up her face. She was teased for how she looked, others claiming she was attempting to go against the sorting and become a Love Interest. In reality, old habits die hard, and her mother had enforced those habits upon her at a young age.

She placed a black knit sweater over her black tank top, gray leggings covered by her combat boots. Throwing her satchel bag over herself, she exited her one-bedroom apartment, locked the door, and left towards Central City.

Even early in the morning, the activities of Central City were starting. A group of three masked men, dressed in black escaped from a club with a black suitcase in the middle one's hands. A man and woman walked side by side, the man picking a flower and placing it into her hair as she blushed. A shadowy figure stood above the city streets, a cape flapping in the wind as they looked on around them.

Jinx stopped at a vendor, another Background Character by the name of Stan operated the cart. He was the fourth generation owner of the cart, having the best coffee in all of Central City.

"Good morning Ms. Dorian." He said with a smile.

"Good morning, Stan, how are you?" She asked kindly.

"Last night I was able to watch a fight between a Hero and Villain, you would not believe what happened!" He exclaimed, filling a medium coffee for her.

"What happened?" Jinx asked giggling.

"They kissed!"

"What?" Jinx asked with wide eyes.

Stan handed her the coffee and Jinx gave him the cash. "No exaggeration Jinx, two masked figures kissing in the rain."

Jinx took a sip of her coffee, the taste dancing across her tongue. "You should sell the story, I'm sure the town would love the drama."

Stan winked at her. "I might just do that."

Jinx smiled thanking Stan for the coffee once again before heading towards the bank. She knew Stan would not try to sell the story, it was not their role in society to inform the papers on things like that. But it wouldn't stop them from gossiping to the other Background Characters.

Climbing the marble steps to the white column fronted bank, Jinx couldn't help but feel as though she was being watched. She looked behind her, but saw no one there. Shrugging it off, she opened the door to the bank, smiling as she saw Peggy, her work best friend.

"I have some gossip to share." Jinx greeted, placing her bag around the back of her chair.

"My ears are ready." Peggy gleamed, wiping down the wooden fronts to the desks.

"Stan, the coffee vendor, he said he saw a Hero and Villain fighting last night." Jinx started.

"Well, Jinx, that is what Heroes and Villains do." Peggy chuckled.

"And then they kissed." Jinx smiled evilly.

Peggy stopped her wiping, mouth dropping open and eyes going wide. "They kissed?"

Jinx nodded, taking another sip from her coffee, a smug smile gracing her lips.

Peggy shook her head, continuing to wipe the counter. "He should sell the story."

"I said the same thing." Jinx laughed. "Do you need your drawer filled? I'm going to fill mine."

"No, no, I already did. Be careful though, the vault door is sticking today." Peggy said.

Jinx nodded, taking her money drawer from its spot and walking behind the teller desks to the hall that led to the vault. One of the lights in the hall was out, Jinx making a mental note to tell the maintenance worker about it later.

She took out her keys, opening the metal cell door that barricaded the entrance to the vault. It unlocked with a loud clang, Jinx opening it and putting in the code to the vault quickly. She felt the hinges click, pulling on the door to reveal the money inside.

There was no sense of organization to the vault. Gold bars, jewels, coins, cash, all placed into somewhat neat piles within. Jinx got on her knees, placing the correct amount of money into the sections of her drawer. As she did, she felt goosebumps rise to her skin, a feeling of being watched more intense now. She snapped her head back, only seeing the clear hallway with the broken light. She shook her head, patching it up to paranoia that Thad is gone.

Jinx stood after filling her drawer, quickly leaving the vault, and securing it tightly. Her footsteps echoed down the hall as she left, retreating into the light where she did not feel so isolated and alone.

The day went on as usual, people coming in to make transactions, Villains and Henchmen trying to rob the bank, their counterpart Heroes saving the day. Jinx was used to having a knife to her throat at this point, some of the Villains being regulars and not handling her so roughly anymore.

As the last customer left for the day, the afternoon sun throwing yellow beams of light into the high windows of the bank, Jinx closed the door. She helped Peggy clean, put away the money left in the drawer and locked everything up. It was nothing unusual for a Wednesday, the same routine would happen on Thursday and Friday, then repeat the whole next week. At least that part of being a Background Character wasn't bad.

She followed the same pathway back to her apartment, made herself a meal, watched a movie, then went to sleep.

However, that night, Jinx had a nightmare.

She couldn't understand fully on what was happening, only that she was standing on the stage again, at her current age. People of all three cities were there, along with two other people. Ren Valder, and Micha Torrance. The nerves rattled within her, the dress she wore the same from that night. It was too much, she had already been sorted, she didn't need this.

"You're a hero, Jinny." Her brother's voice said behind her.

On one side of the stage, Ren stood. His hand was extended, as if offering her to join the Villains. On the other, her parents, Micha, and Thaddeus stood, offering her their hands. She didn't want to choose, she wanted things to stay how they were. She wanted to stay invisible.

"Jinx Dorian. Age: 24. Sorting."

Her alarm went off, Jinx's hand slamming over it as she rolled out of bed. She repeated the same routine as yesterday, ending up sitting behind the teller desk of the bank once again.

"You look off." Peggy said, eyeing her nervously as a customer walked away.

"I just had a weird dream last night, but it's nothing." She smiled.

Peggy opened her mouth to ask more questions when the door to the bank burst open.

"A little late for the first of the day, don't you think?" Jinx asked looking to her watch.

Peggy hummed. "Yeah, that is strange."

A group of men rampaged into the bank, a cloud of smoke following them. Jinx looked at Peggy, both women realizing this was not a lower-level Villain, but a top tier one.

The men were all wearing half faced masquerade masks, donned in suits to match the colors of them. Two of the men came after Jinx, grabbing her by the arms and throwing her to the ground. She slid across the floor where she was picked up again.

She scowled at the men, spitting on the one in front of her. He showed her his teeth in a snarl, his hand rearing back and slamming into her face.

Jinx fell back again, tasting blood in her mouth from the split lip he gave her. He must be new, she would've done whatever if he would've been polite.

"Jinx!" Peggy called out.

Jinx looked up, seeing that Peggy was knelt on the ground, surrounded by two men with a knife to her throat. Tears lined her eyes as she looked to Jinx, more fear than they had experienced in a long time.

"Just do as they say, Peggy." Jinx called out. "We're only Background Characters."

Peggy nodded, her chin quivering.

"Jinx Dorian?" A voice came from beyond the smoke. "The daughter of the Dorian family who was sorted into Background Character?"

Jinx sighed, rolling her eyes. "Yep, that's me."

A man immerged from the smoke, dressed in a fully black suit. He wore a half masquerade mask like the others, only his was checkered with black and white, silver lining the rim. Even through his mask, Jinx could see the unmistakable green eyes that belonged to Ren Valder.

He smirked as he walked towards her, stopping where she knelt to put a black gloved finger beneath her chin. "Background life becomes you, though I do prefer you without the injuries."

"I couldn't agree more, take that up with your Henchman who seems too eager to prove himself." Jinx said sarcastically, narrowing her eyes at the man to her right.

There was a flicker of emotion across Ren's eyes. His hand quickly went to his side, and pulled out a handgun. Jinx closed her eyes shielding her face, as she heard Peggy squeal out in fear.

Jinx had expected to feel the sting of the bullet, but there was no shot fired. Not yet. She peaked open her eyes, noticing the gun was not aimed to her, but the Henchman by her side.

"Rise." Ren said, the barrel of the gun resting on the man's forehead.

The Henchman let go of Jinx, rising to his feet.

"Did you hurt her?" Ren nodded towards Jinx.

"Yes, sir."

"Why?"

The Henchman hesitated, his eyes looking to Jinx with worry. Jinx had no idea what was going on, this was not something she typically experienced as a Background Character. She was scared and unsure of what to do.

"She spit on me, Background Characters don't do that." He commented.

A smile curled on Ren's lips. "Oh, but they do. Especially when you order them to."

Ren's finger pulled the trigger, the bullet going through the man's head as blood sprayed over the floor and Jinx. He made a disgusted face, wiping the gun off on his suit. Another Henchman offered Ren a rag to wipe the blood off his face and hands. Ren holstered the gun in his jacket before looking back to her.

"He won't be bothering you again BC Dorian." Ren smirked, stepping over the body and forcing her up. "Now, let's talk money, shall we?"

He forced Jinx down the hall toward the vault, Jinx opening it without much issue.

"Clear it." Ren order the minions, pulling Jinx to the side and pressing her against the wall. His right hand was flushed against her throat, the left held against the wall. Jinx looked away from him, struggling to breathe through the pressure.

"Now, now, now, I don't like the lack of fear you have, Dorian." He seethed, his face was close to her ear, uncomfortably so.

"I was raised with a Hero father, and sorted into the worst society, I don't fear easy." She struggled to say.

He hummed, his left hand lifting from the wall to trace down her cheek. "I do love when you talk back to me, it's thrilling." She didn't answer, shielding her face away from him. "Maybe I'll take you with me, no one will miss a Background Character."

Jinx felt her heart begin to pound in her chest. A Villain surely wouldn't want her, right? She was nothing, a disgrace among her family, a random face on the street.

"I-I'm not worth it." She squeaked.

The hold around her throat loosened, Jinx looking to Ren. While his lips were still tucked into a menacing smile, there was a pain in his eyes as he looked upon her.

"Boss, we're done!" A Henchman yelled.

The look was gone and Ren released the hold on her neck. Instead, he wrapped his arms around her waist, lifting her over his shoulder.

"Put me down!" She screamed.

"I like you better when you're screaming, Dorian, sounds so much like home." He chuckled.

Jinx kicked and hit against him, trying her best to get out of his hold. He walked them towards the exit, the Henchmen leaving Peggy's side and making their way out.

"Peggy!" Jinx yelled, "Tell the commissioner I was taken by-."

Ren pulled Jinx to the floor covering her mouth with his hand. "So, you do know who I am. I was sure you had forgotten."

The ceiling of the roof caved in, repelling down from it was a man that made both her and Ren groan. Micha Torrance.

Micha was Ren's Hero, his other half. Jinx wasn't sure how the sorting determined Heroes and Villains' their perfect match, but it was always interesting to see them equally powerful. However, Micha was the perfect Hero.

Even in school Micha was bubbly, morally only saw black and white. He led the school in sports, was captain of the football team, even kept his virginity until he knew what his status in society was. Why he kept his virginity was always a question since he lost it soon after, not to his Love Interest, but a random girl.

Now, as he slid down into the bank from the high vaulted ceiling, it was like he expanded. His muscles were giant, his waist thin. His light brown hair fell into a neat swoop over his forehead, his golden brown skin was vibrant, especially paired with his hazel eyes.

He wore a tight, spandex white suit. It had the letter 'M' printed on it in blue, matching the tights he had underneath. Jinx couldn't help but notice the bulge in the pubic area, looking away from it. White gloves covered his hands, and white leather boots, his feet.

"Fret not, I am here to save you." He announced in a mighty tone.

"You couldn't have had any other Hero?" Jinx groaned. "I don't want a picture with him in the paper."

Ren looked at her with a smirk. "You really think I would've chosen him if I had the choice?"

"I mean if I had been his Villain, he would've been dead by now." Jinx muttered.

Ren grinned. "You're definitely coming home with me."

Jinx cursed to herself, wishing she would've kept her mouth shut. She watched as Micha unhooked himself from his repelling gear, standing with his hands on his hips in a traditional Hero stance. Peggy stared at him dreamily from behind, causing Jinx to roll her eyes.

"Release the BC, clown!" Micha said.

Jinx sucked on her teeth. "Clown?"

"He doesn't get many points in creativity." Ren commented.

"What do you call yourself then?" She asked.

"The Jester." He said.

Jinx looked back to him with a raised eyebrow. "Could've done better."

Ren scoffed, focusing his attention on Micha. "This is my prize from Central City, you cannot take her from me."

"You both need acting classes." Jinx muttered, Ren's hand lifting and hitting her in the stomach. Jinx bent over, groaning, before Ren pulled her back towards him.

"She's innocent in this fight, let her-." Micha started.

"Just fucking fight already, I want to go home." Jinx yelled.

The room went quiet, all the occupants looking at her surprised.

"This is bullshit." Jinx mumbled.

Her foot slammed down onto the pointed glossed shoes of Ren, causing him to let her go. She stomped away from the Villain, and towards the back of the teller desks. She sat down, placing her chin in her hand and watched.

Micha looked at her with an open mouth, Ren also having a puzzled expression on his face.

"He took the money, Micha, do something you idiot." Jinx ordered.

Micha shook his head, focusing on Ren when they began to fight. It was incredibly boring to her. So boring, in fact, she began to clean up the bank.

There was no way she would patch up the hole in the ceiling, but she could at least clean up the blood that came from the dead Henchman.

She got up from her seat, filled the mop bucket with water and bleach, then rolled it to the body. She rolled the dead man onto a rug to stop the blood from spilling out of him, then began to mop.

Jinx looked over every now and then at the fight, Micha kicking the Henchman's asses. Ren was gone, though she was used to that from Villains.

The mop water was a dark red, the floor still streaked with the blood. She sighed, looking at her watch to see it was a half an hour past closing time. Micha was still fighting; the Henchmen not ever being knocked unconscious.

Jinx walked to her desk, took out her earrings and slipped out of her heels. The marble floor felt cool through the vinyl stockings she wore as she walked to the fight.

"Jinx, what are you doing?" Peggy asked in a panic.

Jinx shrugged. "Getting us out of here."

Peggy stared at Jinx with an open mouth, watching as she walked into the fight. She punched a Henchman in the mouth, his body going limp as he fell to the floor. The others looked at her, pausing before they swarmed.

She cursed herself for not stretching, not having done many of these moves since she was a teenager practicing with her brother. One by one, the Henchmen fell around her.

Jinx had just finished knocking out another Henchman when she felt a blade to her back and a hand to her throat.

"I think the sorting was wrong about you, Dorian." Ren's voice purred in her ear.

"I think I just want to go home and you are making me stay late." She snapped.

Ren clicked his tongue. "Where have you been all my life?"

"Getting ignored by society." Jinx said, pushing into the knife. "If you're going to stab me, get it over with."

Suddenly, Ren was thrown back, Jinx getting enclosed in Micha's giant embrace. The smell of his sweat hit her nose, her hands pushing away from him.

"Don't worry, you're safe now." He recited.

"Hey, Micha, get off me. You smell horrendous." Jinx protested. Micha loosened his grip on her, Jinx pushing herself from him. "Do you even wash that thing?"

"Uh yes, every Thursday." He said.

"Today is Thursday, have you washed it since last Thursday?" Jinx asked, desperate for a yes she knew was not coming.

When he didn't answer, Jinx rubbed the back of her neck, looking up. She walked away from him and to the satchel bag over her chair. She slipped on her heels, then walked towards the entrance.

"Wait, you can't go!" Micha announced.

Jinx looked at him. "I most definitely can."

"No, you-you have to be my Love Interest." He objected.

Jinx laughed sarcastically. "Sorry, but I'm just a Background Character, no one important."

He took her hand as she turned away. She narrowed her eyes. "Get your hand off me."

"I need to know who you are!" He protested.

"Jinx Dorian, age twenty-four, Background Character." Ren smirked as he got off the floor. "Only daughter of Olivia and Packer Dorian, sister to Thaddeus Dorian."

"If I didn't know any better, I'd assumed you had been stalking me." Jinx stated without emotion.

"Well do you?" He asked.

"Do I what?"

"Know better?"

He grabbed onto her free hand, now making both of her hands occupied by a Villain and a Hero. Jinx opened her mouth, only to close it when she realized she didn't know what to say. She was not supposed to get this much attention, much less from a competing Villain and Hero.

And that is when the police arrived.

"It adds up to what Micha said, though I am going to have to take your word for it on the previous events since Ren won't talk." The commissioner grunted.

Jinx nodded, her knee bouncing. "So what now?"

The commissioner sighed, pressing his fingers to his eyes. "I am going to have you re-sorted. Obviously, there's something else to you that is more than just a Background Character."

"When?" She asked, her heart pounding.

"I'll have an emergency sorting tonight." He said.

Her knee bounced harder, eyes focused on her hands. "I want the two of them to be there." The commissioner furrowed his brows. "Ren and Micha, so they can see I am nothing more than a Background Character."

"Hm, I see why not, although Ren is going to be charged with-."

"We both know he will escape within a day, just let him come." Jinx interrupted.

The commissioner looked to Jinx with furrowed brows, scratching his chin.

"If there's nothing else, I would like to change before the ceremony and tell my parents." Jinx said.

The commissioner nodded his head. "You may leave, but Jinx, in my thirty years of being the commissioner and twelve years of Hero duties before that, I have never once heard a Background Character interrupt me."

Jinx bit her lip, standing. "I'll see you tonight."

She walked towards the door, it opening as she went to leave. She did not look back as the commissioner watched her, nervous he was going to interrogate her further. After all, she wanted to look good for the sorting ceremony.

Chapter Two
A Gray Area

After telling her parents about the sudden sorting ceremony and denying her mother's insistence to help her get ready, Jinx stood in front of the mirror.

She had chosen red, a color that suited her pink skin and allowed for the curves of her body to be adored. She had found the dress she now wore on sale in a Background Character store, definitely put there by mistake. It hugged her body in all the right ways, the neckline showing off her collarbones and the string of pearls she wore. Jinx had left her hair down into curls, similar to the type her mother wore. A maroon lipstick had been carefully placed, matching with the similar shade of eyeshadow she applied. Altogether, Jinx found herself hot.

She slipped on her black stiletto boots, grabbed the small wallet with her identification card in it, and opened the door. Unluckily for her, Micha was standing on the other side with a white button-down shirt and jeans. His hand was raised, posed as if about to knock.

"I, uh, was going to knock." He stuttered, eyes never meeting her face as they ran along her body.

"Uh huh." Jinx said with her eyebrow raised.

"Oh please, don't mind him." Ren said from behind her. "Men can be pigs sometimes."

Jinx turned, Ren placing an arm over her shoulders, making her stand beside him. He wore a dark suit, similar to the one he had on with the mask. It was long and slim fitted, yet perfectly molded to his body.

"How did you get into my apartment?" Jinx asked, looking to the windows behind her, all were shut and locked.

"Shall we?" Ren asked, ignoring her.

Jinx rolled her eyes, praying the attention from these two would stop once she was determined to be just a Background Character again. As she got to the bottom of her stairs, Jinx turned to walk towards Central City Main, only she was stopped.

"Dorian, you can't possibly think we'd let you walk to Central City looking like that did you?" Ren smirked.

Jinx raised an eyebrow at him. "Are you the jealous type, Ren? Because the only thing I could think of stopping me would be you killing other Background Characters."

Micha looked between Ren and Jinx, smiling weakly. "Actually, I thought the heels might hurt."

Jinx looked to Micha, tilting her head to the side. His eyes nervously swept over her, Jinx looking to her feet then back to him.

"You have a car?" Jinx asked.

Micha lifted a key, unlocking a white and blue sports car from behind him. She was grateful for that, she definitely was expecting him to offer to carry her.

"Do you match everything to your outfit you don't wash?" She asked.

His cheeks went red as Jinx walked past him and towards the car. She reached for the handle, but Ren's black gloved hand was already there, opening the door for her. Jinx sighed deeply, sitting herself into the car. The door slammed shut next to her as the driver's side door opened. Micha got in, his large frame sitting surprisingly well in the small car. He started the engine, smiling at her.

"Wait, isn't Ren coming?" Jinx asked.

"He's in his car."

As Micha finished his sentence, a similar car to Micha's pulled up next to them. It was all black with silver around the trim. The window rolled down, Ren smiling at her from inside. She could barely see out the windows from his tint, wondering how he was planning on driving the car when it hit night.

"I'll catch you over there." Ren winked, then took off.

Jinx barely was able to read his license plate:

N0TACL0WN

Jinx couldn't help but giggle, causing Micha to look at her funny.

"Just go." She said with a smile, not wanting to take the time to explain the joke.

As Jinx stepped out of the car, she was assaulted by flashing lights of photographers. She shielded her eyes, trying to adjust to the light blinding her. Big arms then encompassed her, Jinx once again that day having to push Micha off of her. At least this time he didn't smell bad.

"Stop trying to touch me, I'm not your Love Interest." She snapped.

"But I am attracted to you and you make me nervous." He said.

"I'm hot, and you have nerves around women." Jinx said as plainly as she could.

"Plus she's in love with me." Ren smiled, wrapping his arm around her again.

She brushed off his arm, stepping away from both the men. "Fuck, both of you stop touching me."

"Jinny!" Jinx's mom's voice cut through the clamor of people. She turned, seeing her mother and father rushing over to her.

"What is going on?" Olivia asked, hugging Jinx.

Jinx sighed. "I had one crazy day at the bank and now they're resorting me."

"Over a simple attack?" Packard asked suspiciously.

Jinx shrugged. "I may have beat up some Henchmen."

Packard's eyes sparkled. "How many? Two? Four? Six?"

"Please stop counting in twos dad." Jinx forced a laugh.

Jinx saw the commissioner walk toward them, more flashing of cameras going off at his arrival. "It's time, Jinx Dorian."

Jinx nodded, her mother squeezing her hand one last time before latching onto Packard. Nerves bubbled up inside of her as she followed the commissioner to the stage where the blue light waited. Her entourage had followed her, though they stayed in the darkness before the stage as she took the stairs leading up.

The auditorium was empty besides the few people she requested to be there, and the police accompanied by the commissioner waiting for her results. The blue spotlight shown down on Central City's crest, a series of triangular knots, one side thorned vines, the other side covered in roses.

Jinx's breath came out shakily, her hands knotting together as she approached the blue light that once told her all her fears would come true. That she would be nothing and amount to no more than being someone who opens a safe for Villains.

Her heels clacked across the final few steps of the wood, her back straightening and her chin forced up. She faced the audience as the voice announced her.

"Jinx Dorian. Age: twenty-four. Previous sort: Background Character. Sorting."

Her heart raced in her chest as she waited. She looked below the stage to see her parents, holding each other with a hopeful look in their eyes. She then saw Micha, his hopeful look was intense, staring at her like she would be marrying him soon after. And finally, there was Ren. He did not look at her like he was hopeful. It was something different, like he was just going along with it, waiting for her to be finished.

"Sorting completed." The voice said.

The light around her turned white. There was hushed talking from her parents, Micha and Ren looking confused.

"Morally Gray."

Jinx's mouth dropped open, looking to the commissioner who stared at her in awe.

Being Morally Gray was supposed to be a myth, a classification that banished people from Central City. She would rather be a Background Character than this.

"It has to be wrong," Jinx told him, "Do it again."

"The sort is never wrong." He said.

"It was wrong the first time!" She screamed, fear rushing into her as she saw the policemen come onto the stage. "You can't do this."

"I'm sorry, Ms. Dorian, but you have no other half. You're a danger to the city."

Jinx looked to her parents who refused to look to her. She then looked to Micha, who stared at her in horror. She was not a monster; she was not a threat. Why didn't anyone try to defend her?

The light above her turned red, everyone pausing as a hand wrapped around Jinx's waist.

"Ren Valder. Age: twenty-four. Original Sort: Villain."

"Ready for an adventure?" Ren whispered in her ear.

Jinx didn't respond, only turned into him, wrapping her arms around his neck. He was the only thing between safety and banishment.

His hands grabbed under her knees, lifting her into a cradled position.

"Don't open your eyes, Dorian, I don't want you to get sick on my suit." He sneered.

Jinx closed her eyes tight, clutching onto Ren's neck. She felt her whole body jerk in an instant, her stomach flipping and her head pounding.

"You can open your eyes now." Ren said, dropping her knees so that she was standing again.

She slowly opened them, realizing she was no longer on the stage or anywhere she was familiar with. Jinx spun around, her eyes adjusting to the dark.

"Where are w-."

"I told you I'd take you home, didn't I?" Ren smirked.

"Home?" Jinx said, looking around again. "You live here?"

The entire area was dark, water dripping from stalactites above her. There was no doors or rooms, no reasonable way in or out, so how did they get there?

"Technically we are under my home," He said with a smirk. "This is nothing but a cave."

"Then why not take us to your home, and how did we even get here?" Jinx asked.

Ren shook his head. "If I exposed all my secrets to you Dorian, I wouldn't be a very good Villain."

Jinx opened and closed her mouth. She was trapped now. Inside a cave with a Villain who saved her from the supposedly good guys. She would never have her life back that she had before, and who knows if the Villains would allow her to stay in Vileterra.

"You'll be safe here, as ironic as that may sound to you Dorian. You're one of us now." Ren gleamed.

"I'm not a Villain." She objected.

"No, but you have the capacity to become one, which is all they need as an excuse to kill you." Ren grumbled, leaning against a rock wall. "I personally think you are too pretty to die."

Jinx rolled her eyes. "Glad I got something out of being good looking."

Ren smirked. "So, Ms. Dorian, what would you like to do as your first day of being a Villain."

"I'm not a Villain." Jinx objected.

"Yet." Ren winked. "You were outcasted by society, twice now, have a proclivity towards violence and sarcasm, think of your safety above all else, and yet, you claim not to be a Villain?"

Jinx sighed, placing a hand to her head. "Not a Villain because I still want to help people, fuck I wanted to be a doctor before the sorting."

"A doctor?" Ren laughed.

Jinx narrowed her eyes at him. "I wanted to do good, but the sorting told me I was much more suited to be a bank teller. Never mind I had perfect grades, knew three languages, and had an internship lined up at the hospital."

Ren whistled. "And your anger." He circled her, his hand running along the back of her dress. "Another sign of Villainy."

"I'm not a fucking Villain!" She screamed.

The sound echoed through the caves, Ren stopping to look at her. She turned her head away from him, her hands finding each other and a nail digging into her thumb.

"I'm sorry for yelling." She said quietly.

Ren furrowed his brows, putting a finger under her chin and lifting it until her eyes met his. "Never apologize to me."

Jinx nodded, confused as to why Ren was being so nice to her. Even if he was frustrating, he saved her, something Villains didn't do. He also looked at her differently than the people who lived in Honorville, like he was trying to see the real her, not some person who she was supposed to be.

"Come on, I'm going to introduce you to my parents. My dad will definitely get a kick out of your family line." Ren chuckled, pushing a rock on the cave wall.

The rock moved inwards, and the ceiling above her trembled. Ren put his arm around her waist, guiding her to a specific spot as the rocks above her lowered into a staircase. As everything settled, Ren offered his hand forward, implying that Jinx climb the stairs.

"Are your parents going to hate me?" She asked. "I am a Dorian."

Ren smirked. "Because you are a Dorian they'll love you."

Jinx didn't understand what he meant but climbed the stairs. Her only real option was to trust him, she was in a cave with seemingly no other entrance or exit after all. That then led to another question, how did they get there to begin with?

It felt strange knowing she was in the Villain's territory, Vileterra. She had grown up in Honorville, her parents being the top Heroes in their time. But once Jinx had been sorted into Background Character, she had to move to Central City. There was no place for her in Honorville anymore.

However, growing up in Honorville, she had heard stories of the Villain's lairs. How they were dark and dingy, lacking light and life. She had pictured a dungeon of sorts, filled with bones and maybe a few rotting corpses, so that was all she was expecting. When getting to the top of the stairs, Jinx was surprised to see there was not cold, damp halls or spiderwebs in the corners. The house was not run down or empty, but, in fact, it was filled with life.

An orange fire crackled in a hearth that connected through two rooms. It sent an autumn feel throughout the area, complimented by the accented red, brown, and mustard yellows that decorated the rest of the space. Full bodies of armor lined the walls, each having a garland of colored leaves wrapped around them.

A maroon couch sat over a rug, plush blankets draped over the sides, so cozy Jinx felt tired just looking at them. The couch was accompanied by two armchairs with similar blankets displayed over them. Pillows rested on each chair, both saying something involving witches. A rug on the floor was circular, having constellations embedded into it. A glass coffee table was in the middle of the rug, holding coasters and a book on… palm reading?

"My mother was in charge of decorations; she could've had worse tastes." Ren commented.

"Is she a witch?" Jinx asked, intrigued.

Ren chuckled. "She's the Cosmic Sorceress."

Jinx spun, her eyes widened. "Like, Villain who killed their Hero, Cosmic Sorceress?"

Ren nodded. "Let me tell you, she regrets that, says it ruined her fun."

He walked past Jinx and towards a thick wooden door. She followed him, interested to see what the rest of Ren's home looked like. She could barely wrap her head around Ren's mother being the Cosmic Sorceress, someone so powerful.

As they entered a room that looked like a dining room, Jinx recognized his father almost instantly. He had slicked back, black hair, similar to Ren's. His eyes were completely black, no semblance of the whites that were supposed to be present. The tips of his fingers were blackened, along with the veins that ran up his neck and arms. He wore a black suit, cuffed with silver cuff links and a silver embroidered tie.

Ren's father was no other than her own father's Villain half, Demented Doom. It caused Jinx to stop in her tracks, face paling wondering if it was a good idea for her to be here.

The Cosmic Sorceress sat beside him, hand in his. She was elegant. She wore a long black dress with a plummeting neckline. Her body was filled with tattoos, and Jinx swore they moved. Her red hair laid in tight curls, creating a halo around her head. Her green eyes were the same as Ren's, though they sparkled with a power that was absent in his own. Rings decorated her fingers, all more extravagant than anything Jinx ever dreamed of owning.

Ren didn't stop his approach towards his parents, taking a seat across from his mother. His parents looked from each other towards Jinx, her heart pounding in her chest.

"Who's your captive, Ren?" His mother asked, placing a long, sharpened nail to her blood red lips.

Ren looked to Jinx, smirking. "Guess."

His parent's faces lit up with the game, looking over Jinx intensely.

"Micha's Love Interest?" His father guessed. Ren shook his head.

"A Best Friend?" His mother asked. Ren once again shook his head.

"A sibling of some sort?" His father said, narrowing his eyes at Jinx.

"Wrong again." Ren smirked.

His mother gasped, looking to Ren. "Is this a possible Villain you took a fancy to?"

"I do like what I have seen from her, but she is something more than that." Ren smiled evilly. "Any other guesses?"

Jinx watched in horror as they continued to guess who she was, never succeeding in naming her properly, though why would they? Before today, she was only a Background Character. A shame to the Dorian family name.

"You've stumped us, darling, who is she?" His mother concluded with a smile.

"Jinx Dorian, the only daughter of Olivia and Packard Dorian. Once claimed to be a Background Character, now turned Morally Gray." Ren announced.

His mother clapped her hands together, a smile that made Jinx's skin crawl plastered onto her face. Ren's father smiled, a gleam in his eye.

"Years of being Packard's nemesis and my own son had done a better job than I have." He gleamed.

"Come sit down, Jinx, tell us how you came to be Morally Gray." Ren's mother shimmered in a sparkling yellow light. Jinx warily looked to Ren, then to his parents. "Oh, poor thing is probably terrified having grown up in Honorville. Ren, be a gentleman and help her out." His mother pouted.

"Come sit." Ren ordered, a shimmer of green encompassing him.

Jinx was appalled that he would order her like that, though he was a Villain who knew no boundaries.

"How about a please." Jinx stated, her voice not as wobbly as she felt.

There was shock from all three Villains at her retort. Why? She couldn't have guessed.

"I said, sit." He ordered again, this time the glowing was intense.

"Say it with me, p-lee-sss." She said, annoyed this time. Was he trying to show off to his parents? And what was with the green light?

Ren looked to his mother, his brows furrowed. Her eyes glanced to him, then back to Jinx.

"Bow." She ordered. Jinx felt a small prickle against her skin, but rubbing her hand over it, the feeling went away.

"Interesting," Demented Doom whispered. He stood from his place, going to walk to Jinx. Fear paralyzed her as she saw the black tips of his fingers grow up his hands.

Ren stood, stopping his father's advance towards her. "You will not touch her."

Jinx looked to Ren, grateful for the interference, but still confused over the encounter. To her surprise, Demented Doom nodded, though he lifted an eyebrow to Ren. He turned to Jinx, walking towards her. He grabbed her hand quickly, pulled out a chair, and shoved her into it.

"This is my way of saying please." He grumbled.

Jinx pursed her lips looking up to him. "We'll work on your manners."

The Cosmic Sorceress giggled, taking her goblet, and placing it to her lips. "Tell me, Jinx, have you always been immune to magic?"

"What?" Jinx asked.

"It is not everyday that both my and Ren's powers are defenseless against a person, Villain, Hero, commoner. You are a rarity indeed." She said, looking over Jinx with calculated interest.

"I don't understand," Jinx said, "I am nothing special, I was only a Background Character until today."

"A Background Character you say?" Demented Doom pondered. "That must have been a shock to your parents seeing who they are."

Jinx scoffed. "As soon as I was sorted, they had already arranged for my things to be packed and rented me an apartment to live in."

Ren jerked his head back. "As soon as you were sorted?"

Jinx nodded. "To them, I was just a Background Character."

"That's harsh, even for a Villain." Demented Doom said, shaking his head.

Jinx was shocked at their reaction. They were Villains, wouldn't they be the first to encourage pain and agony onto others? Jinx picked at the skin around her nails under the table. Everything she knew in life was turning out to be an illusion, pushed onto her by society and her parents.

"Morally Gray is what you are now considered, correct? You were re-sorted?" Demented Doom asked.

Jinx nodded. "And they tried to kill me for it."

"Well of course they did, Jinx. You are dangerous after all." Cosmic Sorceress said nonchalantly.

"Dangerous how?" She asked.

Ren scoffed. "Did you not pay attention in classes, miss high marks?"

Jinx closed her eyes sighing. "I didn't need my schooling after I was sorted into Background Character, remember?"

Demented Doom chuckled. "A Morally Gray sorting is unique in the fact that you do not have another half. You are a Hero or a Villain, your choice. Because you don't have your other half, you will be unstoppable in whatever you choose, but also tormented with the other part of you trying to come through."

Jinx sat back in her chair. This morning she woke up as someone without any mark to society. A person who unlocked the safe for Villains, cleaned up the bank, and went home. Now, she was the most powerful person in the city.

"The fact Ren most likely saved you is a good thing." Cosmic Sorceress said. "Heroes and police will not step foot in Vileterra, so you will be safe here until you figure out who you are."

"And what if I don't want to be good or evil, what if I want to stay gray?" She asked, not looking up.

Cosmic Sorceress looked to her husband, not having the answer. He shook his head, breathing in deeply.

"You would not be welcomed in Honorville or Central City, so you would have to stay in Vileterra anyway. Your goodness will make you a target here from other Villains-."

"She's staying here." Ren said. Everyone looked to him shocked. "I refuse to let her get hurt due to some stupid societal norm or people believing they can gain a leg up in the world by defeating her." He had a darkness to his voice that shook Jinx. "I claimed her, and she is mine."

Fighting past the unnerving tone, Jinx scoffed. "I am no ones but myself. Claim me if you want, but I will kill you the second you try to use that claim against me."

Cosmic Sorceress bounced in her seat, looking to Demented Doom. "Oh, that's her Villain side. How exciting and fierce."

He nodded approvingly. "We will make you a room and send for your things. As long as you're here, you will be protected, but there is one rule, do not, under any circumstances contact your family."

Jinx furrowed her brows, thinking to Thad. "Why?"

"Contact between Heroes and Villains stay in Central City, once that contact is made outside of Central City, a treaty is broken, and all hell will break loose. The system will collapse."

Jinx frowned but nodded. If she was to protect herself, she needed to see the people of Central City and Honorville as her rivals, including

Thaddeus. She was no longer a nobody to them, but the most wanted Villain. A Villain with no Hero.

"Ren, why don't you escort Jinx to the east tower, I believe that area will suit her needs well." Cosmic Sorceress said with a sly smile.

Ren nodded, having a similar smile and stood from his seat. Jinx followed, looking to his parents.

"Thank you, I'd be in a bad spot without your help."

They groaned, flinching.

"Ms. Dorian, please refrain from your Hero ingrained habits. It's a pitiful display of affection." Demented Doom said.

Jinx bit her lips together, wrapping around her chair to follow Ren to a hall that had been behind them.

"Thanking a Villain? What is wrong with you?" He scolded quietly.

Jinx thought back to her mother slapping her across the face for forgetting to thank someone. "I guess it's just habit."

She did not talk while following Ren the rest of the way, lost in her own swirling thoughts. Jinx was no longer herself. She was no longer in a place where she knew the customs and could function as she was supposed to.

Jinx was Morally Gray and now she had to figure out what that meant. Not only that, but Ren had said he claimed her, what does that mean?

Ren looked back to Jinx, wrapping an arm around her shoulders. "You'll be fine, Dorian. Us Villains aren't as bad as you think."

Jinx nodded, looking into his green eyes. She trusted him, something she would have never believed herself to admit. In a world of Heroes and Villains, who would have thought she would be saved by the bad guy?

Chapter Three
Magick, Knives, and Poison

Ren had led her to a door with silver adornments. It was decorated with flowers stamped into the metal. He clicked open the door, exposing a large circular room filled with books.

Jinx's mouth dropped open.

It smelled like the library in Central City, with at least three stories lined with books. A tall ladder was fastened to a track, allowing for access on the top shelves. A spiral iron staircase led up to another floor, the iron railing twisted. A desk was present, facing the door, a large window behind it. Beyond the window, she saw a garden, glowing plants lighting the area with an eerily blue hue. A sitting area with gray padded chairs was off to the left, side tables that served as additional bookshelves rested beside them. The floor was tiled stone, sparkling with black polished gems within them.

"I'll show you where you'll be sleeping." Ren said, a knowing smile on his lips.

Jinx nodded, still absorbing the miraculous layout of the library. She wound up the spiral stairs, passing a room she could only assume was a closet. Rows and rows of empty shelves ready to host shoes, dresses, and other clothing lining the walls. In the middle, a glass case where purple velvet cushions awaited to hold precious jewels.

She continued to follow Ren, stopping at another silver lined door that he opened before stepping through. This time, the silver was imprinted with beasts and monsters, the handle being a lion amid a roar.

When walking into the room, Jinx covered her mouth.

Unlike her room in Honorville, the room her mother decorated in bright colors of yellow and white, plastering flowers over a canopy bed and tulle curtains to be sure she rose as the sun did, this room was dark.

The walls were a slate gray, the wooden floors stained a blackened color. The bedframe was a similar make of the floor, a canopy curtain of black silk tied to each bed post with silver rope. A gray and black quilt covered the bed, a small pillow in the shape of a ghost fronting the mountain of pillows that matched the comforter. The curtains were pulled to the side, held behind a metal hook. A black, shag rug was tucked beneath the bed, extending towards a vanity with a wrought iron mirror pointing at the bed.

Jinx shuttered, knowing she would have to cover the mirror before dressing.

"Everything to your liking?" Ren asked.

"This is all mine?" She asked, spinning to look at him.

He smirked, looking her up and down. "Unless you'd prefer to share it."

She rolled her eyes, biting the corner of her lip. "I don't have to change the colors or make things brighter?"

Ren furrowed his brows. "No? Why would you?"

Jinx shook her head, the corners of her mouth twitching in a smile as she looked over the room again. This room was hers as long as she wanted it. She did not have to pretend to like the colors, or leave the comfort of her pajamas to find a book to read.

"What are you thinking?" Ren asked, a quizzical look over his face.

"When I was growing up, I had to force myself to like bright colors as I was expected to be a Hero. But I adored the darkness of black, gray, and maroon. I'm just pleased I don't have to change." She admitted, walking to sit on the bed. The softness of it encompassed her, and she fell back into it, closing her eyes. "Oh, this is so much better than the bed in Central City."

Ren chuckled from the doorway. Jinx cracked an eye open, looking to him. "What's so funny?"

He shook his head. "It's interesting watching you. You have so many emotions going through you, but you choose to focus on the small things, like the comfort of a bed."

Jinx lifted herself, leaning back on her hands. "I wasn't allowed to think of these small things, Ren. You don't understand half of what I'd gone through in preparation to be a Hero I was never meant to be."

"So tell me." He said, walking towards her.

"What?" She asked, surprised he wanted to know.

"I want to know what makes you tick, Dorian. How your brain works." He pulled out the chair to the vanity, sitting on it backwards with his arms resting on the back. "Not everyone is Morally Gray, you know."

She shook her head. "I don't even know where to start."

"When you first started your Hero training." He said, eyes fixated on her.

Jinx looked down at her hands, grimacing. "I guess it started as soon as I learned to walk."

"My mother, being a Love Interest, had her hopes that I would be just like her. So I was in dresses, learned to do my own hair and makeup by the time I was thirteen. My father, on the other hand, was convinced I was going to be a Hero, forcing me to train harder than any of my other classmates."

"I do remember you in dresses a lot." Ren commented.

Jinx nodded her head to the side. "In all honesty, I hated dresses. I much rather preferred jeans and a sweater, but that was not my right to choose." She rubbed the back of her neck, feeling the string of pearls still on her throat. She reached up, unhooking the gems and placing it to the side.

"The issue with my training is that I was not graceful in the slightest. My footwork was always wrong and to improve that, my father would discipline me, like all fathers do I suppose."

"Discipline you?" Ren asked darkly.

"It was my fault really, and it helped in the long run. If I tripped, I got a lashing. It scarred sometimes, but mother said if I was able to get kidnapped by my Hero's Villain, I could blame it on that." Jinx shook her head. "Sometimes I would be whipped so hard my back would be bloody. A Background Character employed by the family would have to put bandage over my back to keep from the blood seeping into my clothes. That's why I tried so hard, to make my parents proud."

Ren looked uncomfortable, his fist clenching.

"I'm sorry, I can stop." She said.

"No," He said, "Keep going."

"When Thaddeus was sorted as a Hero, my parents really focused on me being Central City's angel. I showed up to all the events, always looking my best, never speaking unless spoken to. They were convinced I was a Love Interest at that point."

"And then I was sorted. Thaddeus was the only one to help me transition, and it was hard. All I knew how to do was look nice, do as I was told, and follow my own path. I didn't know how to cook, clean, wash my clothes, all of that was done for me. But, I survived and faded into the background."

"I was forgotten by my parents for the most part, they did not speak with me unless I initiated it. In fact, the re-sorting was the first time I had seen them in almost two years."

"They abandoned you." Ren stated, his jaw tight.

Jinx shrugged. "I don't blame them. They had an appearance to keep up, even Thaddeus visiting me was looked down upon."

"And you worked at the bank all this time?" Ren asked.

Jinx nodded. "Everyday was the same routine. Get up, get ready, get my coffee, open the bank, close the bank, go home, eat, then sleep."

"Everyday?" Ren asked shocked.

"Except weekends, I wouldn't have anything to do then." She said absentmindedly.

Ren shook his head, looking down in his lap. "I should've come sooner."

"What do you mean?" Jinx asked.

"Nothing." Ren said gruffly. "Goodnight, Dorian. I'll see you tomorrow."

Ren removed himself from the vanity's chair, pushing it back into place. He walked to the door, closing it, leaving Jinx alone in the room. She bit her lip, wondering if she said something wrong. Her mother did tell her to only speak to a Villain if to save your own life, but what life did she have now?

Jinx got up, placing the pearl necklace onto the vanity. She looked at herself in the mirror, not recognizing the face looking back at her. She didn't know who she was supposed to be if not sorted into a specific category. What was her role as Morally Gray?

She sighed, taking an extra blanket she found in a trunk by the door and placing it over the reflective surface. It was a habit she had as a child, letting her ignore the memories of the scars she had on her back. What she didn't admit to, was sometimes it wasn't only during training or when she made a mistake. Sometimes, the whippings were due to Ren's father besting her own.

She refused to tell Ren that though, what would he think of his father or her own when it was the dynamic they played in society?

Jinx slipped off her heels, rolling down her stockings and slipped under the covers. While she normally would've undressed from the constricting clothing, she didn't have any other option to change into.

She closed her eyes, her consciousness fading, the last image going through her mind being Ren's green eyes.

Even with the curtains closed, Jinx still woke up as the sun was peaking over the mountains in the distance. She never remembered there being mentions of mountains in Vileterra, but then again, everything she knew was wrong.

As she walked down the spiral staircase, she was shocked to see her wardrobe had been neatly organized in the giant closet. Within, she also noticed some new clothes, sweaters that were colored in variations of gray, black and maroon, and also jeans, ones she had never seen before.

She smiled weakly, picking up a pair of black jeans and a gray sweater. Retreating to her room, she put on the clothes, a feeling of comfort washing over her. She managed to find a hair tie in the vanity, throwing her hair into a ponytail and letting two pieces hang down at the sides of her face.

Jinx hopped down the stairs, looking over the books and deciding she needed to climb the ladder to see what was at the top. As she ascended, she realized the books got older as she went up, the language and grammar changing in the worn titles.

Formalities of a Vyllain. Heartbreak and the Soule. Terrore.

Magick, Knives, and Poison.

Jinx raised her eyebrows, looping her arm around the wrung of the ladder, pulling out the book. It was bound in purple leather, only the title written in gold lettering found upon it.

She tucked the book in her arm, carefully going down the ladder. As her feet hit the floor she opened up the book, casually walking towards the gray chairs. She sat down, tossing her leg over the arm rest, flipping through the pages.

It was not like the books in Central City, where those books were in pristine condition, this one was old. Pages were loose, the binding barely holding the cover onto it. Brown stains marked some pages, an overall stiff and yellow pigment to them. The language was in the old writing, pictures of plants, daggers, and recipes were listed within. There were also incantations, each stating what they do beforehand.

Gain influynce. Breathe Fyre. Summen Death.

But one really caught her eye. *Water to Wyne.*

Jinx's eyes looked to a vase of water, holding bright red roses. She padded over to it, looking at the book as she read.

"*Aqua ad vinum*

O quam devine

Et magick pretium stipendium

Est autem quaedam mortis vitae."

Jinx waited, but the water stayed clear, not even a red tint to the liquid. She tried again, still nothing. She huffed, tossing her hip out, placing a hand on it while the other held the book open.

"It was a good attempt, but if you wanted wine, you could have just asked." Ren's voice said.

Jinx looked up, her cheeks heating at her embarrassment. Ren leaned against the doorframe, wearing a black t-shirt and black pants. His hair was not slicked back, but roamed free, a gentle wave to the locks.

She bit her lip, but her stomach swirled with nerves. He was very attractive.

"Now the way you're looking at me, that is some magic I hadn't expected this morning." He wiggled his eyebrows.

"I don't know what you're talking about." Jinx spit, turning back to the chair and glancing over the book.

She heard Ren's footsteps get closer, but he did not approach her. Instead, he stopped by the vase, touching one of the flowers.

"Aqua ad vinum

O quam devine

Et magick pretium stipendium

Est autem quaedam mortis vitae."

She looked up to see the rose he touched die in his fingers. The water however, began to change colors, turning a soft pink. He removed the other flowers, bringing the vase to Jinx with a smirk.

"I thought it only right to produce a rosé, given the flowers."

Jinx sat up, placing the book on the table looking at it.

"Go on, take a sip."

He offered Jinx the vase. She took it warily, placing the glass to her lips and letting the contents cascade over her tongue. She looked at him with wide eyes, it was the best rosé she had ever consumed.

"Thing about that spell," He said taking a seat in the unoccupied chair, "What you just tasted is still water. You will get drunk, don't get me wrong, but you will not become dehydrated off of it."

"Why did the rose die?" Jinx asked.

Ren smiled. "A translation to the spell reads; Water to wine, Oh how divine, The magick price to pay, Is the death of living kind."

"In order for the spell to work, you need to sacrifice a living thing?" Jinx asked.

"Exactly." Ren said.

Jinx nodded, looking down at the wine in her hands. She hadn't expected to be able to control magic or produce it, but seeing Ren do it so easily, she wanted to.

"I want to bring you to our weapon stores." Ren said suddenly. "While it seems you are immune to magical attacks, I assume you aren't from physical seeing as you still have that split lip."

Jinx's tongue ran over the scab that had settled onto her lip, she had forgotten all about it.

"What would a weapon do for me, you said I'm safe here." Jinx protested.

"You're safe in my home, but you can't stay cooped up in here forever, Dorian." Ren said with his eyebrow raised. "I personally won't allow it."

Jinx stood, pursing her lips to conceal her smile. "Trying to get rid of me already, Mr. Valder?"

Ren rushed to her, his foot placed behind hers, making her fall back onto the chair. He slid his knee between her legs, his hand encompassing her throat.

"Ren-."

"Let's address a few things," Ren said, his voice riddled with a growl. "I will never abandon you. No matter what you do or what side you choose, I claimed you, so you are mine." Jinx's breath caught in her throat, Ren's green eyes intensely focused on her. "The second, never call me Mr. Valder unless you plan on me fucking you until you can't take anymore."

Jinx gasped, startled by his admission. "But you call me by my last name."

His eyes flicked to her lips, then back to her own gray eyes. "An open invitation when you're ready."

Jinx's mouth dropped open, her face heating. His hand released from her neck, his body moving away from her.

"Shall we, Dorian?" He smirked as if the previous event never happened.

Jinx nodded, standing, following him out the door. As she walked behind him, she placed the back of her hand to her cheek, trying to soothe her burning. As much as she hated to admit it, Jinx knew that Ren meant it when he said he claimed her and at that moment she was okay with that. If she knew one thing about Villains, it was that they always get what they wanted.

Jinx bit at her lip, picking at her cuticles. Even given the danger that put her in, Jinx couldn't help but like it.

Chapter Four
Top of the Class

The weapons room was not as big as Jinx was imagining for a Villain's home. It was no bigger than her own room, though the walls were covered with all sorts of guns, swords, maces, clubs, really anything she could think of. It was strange for her to have so many options, her father mainly forcing knives and guns upon her.

Ren walked towards a glass case, much like the case that was in her closet, and opened the lid. She walked to him, peering inside and seeing the most dazzling collection of daggers she had ever seen.

"Pick one." He said.

Jinx furrowed her brows, looking to him then to the case. "I can't just take a knife."

"You're not taking it; I'm gifting it to you." He chuckled.

Jinx's eyes shot to him; his gaze fixated on her. It made her feel pressured; she also did not want to refuse a gift. Last time she had, it ended badly for her.

She looked over the blades, her eyes fixating on one. It was black with silver flowers covering the hilt and sheath. She picked it up, exposing the blade where she was shocked to see that it too was black, the middle having a silver diamond.

"Is that the blade you choose?" He asked.

Jinx's mouth twitched upwards. It was beautiful, polished, and proper, but had a dark side that was overlooked until it was too late. It was her perfect match. "Yes."

"Good, now let's see if you know how to use it."

Jinx turned, Ren taking a different knife from the case, unsheathing it, and pointing it at her.

"I don't want to hurt you, but I need to see how weak you became as a Background Character." He smiled maliciously.

Jinx narrowed her eyes, removing the dagger from its sheath and getting into a fighting stance.

Ren's eyes looked up and down her body with a watchful stare. Nodding, he lunged at her. She dodged the attack, taking the hand with the knife and pulling him forward while she ran behind him. He stumbled, looking back at her with raised eyebrows and a cocky smile.

"Not bad, Dorian, but what of your actual combat skills?"

"I was taught to avoid fighting as much as I could until I had no choice." She spit.

"But you are not a Hero anymore, you're a Villain, at least in their eyes." Ren said.

Jinx stiffened, Ren taking the opportunity to stab at her again. She used her arm to block his blade, stabbing at him herself. He spun out of her attack, his knife coming down at her.

She twisted, grabbing behind the elbow of his knife's hand, forcing the knife under her arm. She forced him to the floor, kicking out his legs, pressing her knife to his throat.

Ren smiled at her, causing her to remember she was not in an actual survival situation, she wasn't going to get hurt if she lost.

"Reminds me of our school days."

Jinx furrowed her brows. "What do you mean?"

He shook his head. "Don't tell me you forgot training class when we were sixteen. We were paired due to our fathers being enemies. You fought so well, you pinned me to the floor in seconds, a training blade to my throat." He bit his lip. "I knew that if you had been my Hero I would've gladly lost every time just to see you on top of me like that."

Jinx got off him abruptly, walking towards the case. She sheathed the dagger, clutching it tightly in her palm. "I was either the best or I brought shame to my family, Ren." She turned to look at him, rising from the ground. "The teachers were Best Friends and Love Interests, if I failed, especially to you, I would've had to face the consequences at home."

Ren's jaw tightened as he stood, his eyes looking down. She cursed herself for telling him, she needed to keep quiet. She didn't know why it always slipped out around him, the trust she had in Ren was so unnatural it was difficult to navigate.

"Did you think of me?" Ren said, causing Jinx to hesitate.

"Think of you?"

"After school, did you think about me?"

Jinx chuckled. "Yeah actually. I threw out the dress I wore at the sorting ceremony because of you."

Ren furrowed his brows. "Why?"

"The way you looked at me that night while you were on the stage." Jinx shook her head. "I never felt so self-conscious wearing something before."

Ren huffed. "You thought I didn't like your dress?" He reached his hand up, pushing his fingers through his hair.

"Of course, I did, you laughed at me when you saw me." She said, confused.

He shook his head. "I think about you in that dress all the time, Dorian. Not to make myself laugh, but to remember how it felt to not be able to make you smile."

Jinx rubbed her forehead. "You don't make any sense, Ren. We barely knew each other, your idea of me is nothing of who I am really. Fuck, if you liked me so much, why did you wait six years before breaking into my bank?"

Ren's lips lifted in a snarl. "Because your Hero brother was always waiting around you."

"Thaddeus?" Jinx asked, furrowing her brows. "He was off doing other things, never had anything to do with me except when he went off on a quest."

Ren smirked, walking to lean against a wall. Something about the smile made Jinx uneasy. "Keep telling yourself that, Dorian. Your brother is a pain in my ass, I won't lie about that."

Jinx pursed her lips. "And you're a pain in mine, but we won't talk about that."

Ren clicked his tongue. "Oh, come on now, don't be like that. Either way you would have ended up with me."

"No, I wouldn't have. I was a Background Character, Ren, you're a Villain with no reason to see me again after sorting, except to rob the bank."

Ren lost his smile, the nerves twisting in Jinx's stomach.

"Are you hungry? You haven't eaten today."

She watched as he walked towards the door, and waited in the hallway for her. Jinx quickly walked to the hall, not wanting to keep him waiting.

"What is your favorite food?" He asked.

Jinx shook her head, confused. "Um, I don't know what it's called."

"Describe it to me." Ren said.

"Mashed potatoes, corn, carrots, with ground beef and gravy all mixed together."

Ren smiled. "Shepard's pie without the crust. I can manage that."

Jinx hesitated. "I don't know how comfortable I feel with Henchmen making my food, I'd prefer to do it myself."

Ren laughed. "I will be making your food, we only employ Henchmen for dirty work in Central City, otherwise we do everything else ourselves."

"Everything?" Jinx asked with wide eyes.

Ren nodded his head to the side. "We do hire a cleaning lady, but yes."

Jinx stared at him in shock. She had never expected Villains, especially ones that live in such a big manor, to not have servants.

She followed Ren to the kitchens, where he pulled out a high-top chair for her to sit in. He began removing all the ingredients he needed, Jinx unable to follow his quick movements.

"Can I ask you a question?" Jinx asked, resting her head in her hands.

"I will tell you anything you want to know." Ren gleamed.

"How did we end up in that cave so quickly?" The question had been eating her alive.

"Teleportation." Ren said casually.

Jinx lifted her head. "You can teleport?"

Ren nodded, sliding a bunch of potatoes into a boiling pot of water. "I suspect you have a defense magic when you were sorted as well, which is why I cannot order you around."

"Is that what you and your mom were doing last night?" Jinx asked.

"Attempting to, your barrier is strong." Ren tossed her a carrot, Jinx catching it out of habit, looking to it. He then popped one of his own into his mouth. "I've been practicing magic for years under my mother's guidance, so I have to say I'm pretty good."

Jinx bit into her carrot, smiling slightly. It was so strange to be sitting in a kitchen with a Villain making her favorite meal.

"I wish I could've learned magic, it would've been very useful." She said.

"Always time to start." Ren winked.

"And would you be the one teaching me?" She teased.

He looked her up and down, pointing a butcher knife at her. "I think I would get too distracted."

Jinx looked down at her sweater and jeans, furrowing her brows. "Do you have a thing for modest women."

"No, I have a thing for you."

Jinx opened and closed her mouth, blushing. Ren carried about his cooking, though she saw the proud smile he had over his lips.

"Why'd you decide to have a thing for me?" Jinx choked.

"A Villain going after the daughter of a Hero, especially his father's nemesis? It's only in my nature." He sneered.

So, it was only about her father. Jinx was disappointed, hoping it was actually her who was interesting for once. She took another bite of her carrot, trying to hide the disappointment.

Suddenly, there was a breeze that pushed back the loose strands of her hair.

"I was only joking." Ren whispered in her ear. "I've had my eye on you for a long time, Dorian."

The blush came back to her face, heating her neck. She hated how he was so easily able to do that to her. She thought back to their encounter at the bank, how he had pinned her to the wall. The heat to her face and neck intensified.

"Doing okay over there?" Ren asked, his eyebrows raised.

"Um, yeah, just thinking." Jinx said, nervously tucking her hair behind her ear.

"Do that again." Ren said, walking to lean his arms on the counter.

"Do what?" She asked.

"Tuck your hair behind your ear."

Jinx furrowed her brows, untucking the hair and folding her hands together on the counter. "No."

Ren licked his lips, biting the upper one while he nodded. "You'll be the death of me." He muttered.

"Honestly, Ren, you don't make any sense in your conversations sometimes." Jinx said rolling her eyes. "You go from hostile, to flirting, to threatening, it's all very sporadic."

Ren put a large bowl down in front of her, handing her a spoon. "All I want is your confusion." He grinned. "Then you won't think of ways to leave."

Jinx snorted. "You forget that I am your *willing* prisoner. I know nothing of Vileterra, and I am a Dorian."

She lifted the spoon, blowing on it.

"If you would like," Ren said softly, "I can show you the wonders that is Vileterra."

"Is that smart?" Jinx asked.

"You're the smart one, you figure it out." Ren smirked.

Jinx didn't know if she should or not. She technically was an outlaw, a Villain in her own way. However, she carried the Dorian name making her a target. Would Ren protect her if she was to encounter some Villains who weren't as courteous?

"Let's do it." She said, taking a risk.

Ren nodded. "I'll have a dress sent for you to wear."

"A dress?"

He chuckled. "I am not taking you to a random club, Dorian. I'm a high-class Villain, we're going to a ball."

Jinx coughed up some of the water she had been drinking. "A Villain ball. You want to take me, a daughter of Honorville, to a ball with high-ranking Villains."

"You scared?" Ren asked, a malicious smile spreading across his face.

Jinx clenched her jaw. "No." She placed the spoonful of food into her mouth, immediately forgetting all about the Villain ball.

She looked down at the plate, wondering how he had gotten it to taste so good. Not even the servants at her home in Honorville had been able to make it taste this good.

"What did you do to it?" She asked after swallowing.

"Nothing, just cooked it." Ren smiled, absorbing the light that danced in Jinx's eyes.

"It's marvelous." She said through a mouthful of potato.

"I'm glad you approve." He smiled. "If you ever want anything, tell me and I will make it for you."

"Anything at all?" Jinx smiled.

"Anything." Ren said sincerely.

Jinx placed another mouthful of potatoes in, twisting the spoon upside down.

"And what is it you expect in return?" She asked pointing the spoon at him.

"A smile. Once a day will be enough. Not a faked one, but a genuine, real smile." He said.

Jinx paused, looking down. "I can't promise that."

Ren smirked. "Then I will do my best to make it happen."

She looked to him, his green eyes pinned to her. She bit her lip, looking away. "Do you do this to all your captees?"

"Do what?"

"Woo them with gourmet comfort food and tell them pretty lies?"

Ren smirked. "Eventually you'll see that I would never lie to you, not even for the smallest reason."

Jinx shook her head. "Everyone lies, Ren, especially Villains."

"We'll see about that." He said, walking around the counter and towards the door.

"Where are you going?" She asked, more panic in her voice than she would've liked.

He looked over her, a flash of concern in his eyes. "I told you, I'm going to pick you out a dress. I will be back for you, Dorian, don't worry."

He smirked, walking out of the door, leaving Jinx alone in the kitchen. She looked back to the food, shoving another spoonful into her mouth.

Fuck him for making such good food.

Chapter Five
The Villain Ball

When Jinx finally found her way to her room, after many failed attempts, she picked up the book she had been reading earlier. It was fascinating, much more interesting than the books her family had allowed her to read. She absorbed the information like a sponge, learning about a specific sort of plant that looked withered during the day, but bloomed at night, glowing blue. She wondered if those were the flowers in the garden outside the library window.

It was called *venenum flos* or "poisonous flower". It acted as a sedative in small doses, but enough of it and it decomposed the body until there was nothing left.

It was strange to her that such a flower was present outside her window. She was nervous about it since she was in the home of three notorious Villains. But wasn't she one herself? Sure, she was Morally Gray by sorting, but it was the Villains who were protecting her, not the Heroes she had grown up to believe were good.

She continued reading, learning how to prepare such a flower. If Jinx was a Villain now, she would learn the ways of a Villain. Her Hero training was ingrained into her as a child, so she needed to know this if she was Morally Gray anyway.

She flipped through the pages, reading the passages slowly in order not to miss any details. Who knew when this would become useful to her.

Steps coming from the stairs startled her, Ren smiling at her as she sat up.

"How did you—oh, teleportation." She said.

He poked a finger at his nose. "You're catching on, my dear."

Jinx rolled her eyes, laying back into the chair as she had been before. "Did you find me a dress?"

"Of course, I did, and I have no doubt you will outshine every Villain at the ball." He said casually sitting in a chair.

He had changed his clothes back into the original black suit she had met him in. His hair was slicked back, the locks ending at the base of his head.

"You're staring." He said with a cocky smile.

"When did you change?" She asked.

"Before I left. I do have an appearance to keep up." He said.

Jinx chuckled. "You sound like my mother."

Ren raised his eyebrows. "You seem to forget that both of our families are influential in our perspective societies."

She bit her lip, remembering how her mother had scolded her for wearing her hair up while going to school. "Trust me, I haven't forgotten. I only got used to being a Background Character and thus ignored."

Ren looked at her, leaning sideways in her chair with her legs over the armrest. "Trust me on this, Dorian, you were not ignored completely."

"*You* don't count, stalker." She jeered.

He clicked his tongue, looking away from her. "You have no idea."

Jinx furrowed her brows, but ignored the comment, not looking to get anymore information of his supposed stalking.

"Well," She said, slamming the book shut, "Let's see what you picked out for me."

"It's on your bed." Ren said casually.

Jinx stood, walking up the stairs, excited to see what a Villain had chosen to dress her in. She had always dressed according to her mother's preference, but now in Villain territory, what was she to expect?

On her bed, Ren had laid out a beautiful gown. She quickly put it on, only to be disappointed. She wouldn't be able to wear it.

It was black, the dress hugging her curves only to flow outwards towards the back, leading into a short train. The sleeves were long, a loop at the top where she placed her middle finger. The neckline plummeted down to the bottom of her sternum, the dress formed in such a way it pushed her breasts together. Everything about the dress was beautiful, except for the back. It was opened, diamond lined chains swooping across the exposed skin. But she could still see her skin.

The skin was raised and indented, deformed and unattractive. It showed the history of her errors in training, the pain and trauma she did not want anyone to see. Even when loosing her virginity, she kept on a shirt, refusing to turn her back on the man in case he saw it lift ever so slightly.

She felt defeated, sitting on the chair by the vanity, her hand grazing the scars. Jinx would never be able to ignore them, a permanent reminder of what she was supposed to learn. To be obedient and serving.

"Ren, I can't wear this," She called down to him, trying to hide the sorrow in her voice. "It doesn't fit."

She heard his steps coming up the stairs, quickly finding a robe and placing it over her. She felt so stupid, ashamed to hide herself when she was supposed to be perfect.

"Can I come in?" He asked from outside the door.

"I'd prefer if you didn't." She said back, hoping he would leave.

He was Ren, so he came in anyway. He looked her over, furrowing his brows. "Take off the robe, I need to see where it doesn't fit for next time."

Jinx clenched her jaw. "Don't make me."

"Dorian, take off the robe." He ordered.

He didn't need magic for her to obey him, embarrassed as she lowered the robe, facing him. Ren looked over her, his lips pursing.

"It looks fine to me." He said.

"It-It's the back. I don't like how it's exposed." She said quietly.

"Show me." He said softly.

Jinx looked up, hating the conversation she knew she was about to subject herself to. She had told Ren about the discipline, but he wasn't prepared to see it. No one was.

Slowly she turned, her arms crossing over her body to shield herself. She lowered her head, closing her eyes as she waited for his disgust. Only it didn't come.

A warm hand brushed beneath the jeweled strings, rubbing along the scars that rested there. The touch was gentle as if her scars would still feel pain if he pressed too hard.

She pulled away from his hand, turning to face him, though her eyes couldn't meet his. Jinx didn't want to see the look on his face.

"I can't wear this because everyone will see." She whispered. "I can't have them see what was done to me."

Ren walked from her, Jinx closing her eyes and shaking her head. She knew he wouldn't accept her, at least not this part of her.

A vase smashed on the other side of the room, Jinx jerking her head up. The black flowers were spread under the gray shards of glass, water in a puddle beneath it. She turned her head to Ren. His jaw was tightened, lips forced into a thin line. Veins popped from his neck and temple.

"Ren?" Jinx asked weakly.

He looked to her, a fire in his eyes that scared her. The green in them was darker, almost like he was being consumed by something else.

"I am going to kill your father." He snapped.

Jinx's eyes widened; she had not expected that response.

"You can't," She said, "He isn't your Hero, you aren't matched."

"I don't give a shit," He snarled, "He can't get away with hurting you."

"He won't, but you can't go after him when you're angry like this, your mind is clouded." Jinx objected.

He turned from her, pacing in the room while running his hand through his hair. Jinx was nervous on what he was going to do, she didn't know if she could stop him when he could teleport. Then there was the issue of the supposed treaty. Would he risk breaking it just to kill her father?

Jinx sat on the edge of her bed, not sure what to do. "I won't allow you to kill him."

"You couldn't stop me if you tried." He grumbled.

Jinx sighed. "I can't let you because I need to be the one to do it."

Jinx had never spoken those words allowed before, but it was the truth. She resented her parents, playing a part that she knew they had expected from her. When being sorted, she wanted anything but a Background Character because she knew there was a chance to be captured. In that possibility, she could place her father in danger, and keeping with the Hero image, he would risk his life for her.

She would've worked with a Villain to achieve that goal, playing a new role as the grieving daughter.

Ren looked at her with shock, going to sit beside her on the bed. "Did you have a plan?"

She nodded. "I've had one since school."

"But you were sorted into Background Character, so you couldn't follow through." He said, looking up.

"As you said, our family has to keep up appearances, and my appearance was to be invisible." She said.

He smiled, though it did not meet his eyes. "But you're not a Background Character anymore."

She shook her head. "While I was sorted into Morally Gray, they had made me into a Villain."

He lifted an eyebrow, licking his lips. "A Villain? Jinx Dorian, Villain, who would've guessed."

"I guess it was meant to be," She smirked, "After all, you did seek me out."

"Everyday you get more and more attractive." He laughed, standing and holding out a hand. "Ms. Dorian, I believe you should show off your scars tonight. Let everyone know what a Hero can do to their own kin."

Jinx took his hand, standing, feeling uncomfortable with the idea, but nodded. "We do have to keep up appearances."

Ren had teleported them outside of a grand building. It was tall with the front being made mostly of windows. Black marble steps led up to giant double doors, held open by two Henchmen in masks. There were no other buildings around the structure, the only thing around them was black coarse rock.

"What is this place?" She asked.

"Mason Beckard's ballroom." Ren said casually.

"And Mason Beckard is who?" Jinx snorted, annoyed he assumed she knew every Villain.

Ren smirked. "Minor Villain who extorts money and commits fraud. Second richest family in Vileterra."

Jinx nodded. "Who's the first?"

"Mine."

Ren had placed a cloak over her, the hood lined with white fur. He had a matching jacket, his black suit not changing except for diamond cuff links he had fastened before they had left.

She had done her hair in loose curls, pulling some of it up into two ponytails to give her some extra dimension. Ren had insisted she wear a small diamond tiara he had claimed to pick out for this exact occasion. After much arguing, she relented. It did pull the outfit together marvelously, a small row of diamonds embedded into the bottom, topped with beautiful tear drop ones. She also donned a pair of diamond earrings, and while she had protested against Ren giving her so many pieces of jewelry, she enjoyed being pampered.

People already stared at them as they walked up the steps, her arm interlaced with his.

"They're watching." Jinx said in a hushed tone.

Ren smirked. "Of course they are, you are a Morally Gray Dorian, rescued by a devilishly handsome Villain."

Jinx raised her eyebrows. "Is that how you refer to yourself?"

"Am I wrong?"

While she wouldn't admit it to his face, he was not.

Inside, Ren stopped them by two Henchmen taking off his coat. Jinx went to unclasp her own, Ren's hands stopping hers.

"As long as I am around, you will not touch your coat."

Jinx blushed, but allowed him to undo the hooks that held it there, his fingers brushing softly over her neck. He walked around her, removing the coat and folding it over his arm.

The hushed whispers started almost immediately as soon as Ren moved from her back, Jinx holding her head up to fight against the stares.

Ren smiled at her, offering her a hand that she willingly took.

"They saw my back." She whispered.

"They only saw your beauty." He soothed.

He led her into a giant ballroom, easily the size of her childhood home in Honorville. It was circular with a domed ceiling. There were paintings on the ceiling, depictions of bloody sword fights between angels and demons. In the center a golden chain dropped down to a chandelier easily the size of her bedroom.

The walls were painted black, trimmed with a dark gold that matched the chandelier. Alternating black and gold columns lined the room, holding up a second story balcony where some Villains looked out over the dance floor. The floor was a mosaic of marble, plants colored in gold and black she recognized from the book she had read earlier, all poisonous. They pointed towards the center of the room, where a large circular crest presented itself.

"Mr. Ren Valder, it has been a long time since you have presented yourself at one of my parties." A short man with a gray beard and hair said, approaching them.

He had a long, pointed nose, and a potbelly. His suit was formal, a pocket watch chain clipped to the overcoat and tucked into a small pocket to his side. He wore a monocle, though instead of a clear glass, it was tinted red.

"Mason, I felt it was time to show my face to the people again." Ren smiled, though it was not like the one she was used to.

"Indeed, and who is this young woman on your arm?"

Jinx didn't smile, only looked to the man, Mason, with a neutral expression.

"This is Miss Jinx Dorian, I'm sure you have heard about her." Ren said with a sly smirk.

Mason's eyes went wide, his eyes flicking to Ren nervously. "The Morally Gray woman, correct?"

"The very one." Ren said with pride.

"It is a pleasure, Ms. Dorian, though I'm sure many of my guests will be off put by your presence tonight." Mason said.

Jinx couldn't help the snarl that tugged at her lip. "Do you address all your new guests with this level of disrespect?"

Mason's eyes went wide, Jinx catching a poorly hidden smile from Ren.

"No, no, my apologies, I didn't mean any offense." He stammered.

"I am neither a Hero nor Villain, so keep that in mind when addressing me." Jinx spit.

Mason nodded, looking once again to Ren. "Please enjoy."

Ren led Jinx towards a column in the middle of the room, allowing her to be tucked between him and it.

"If I didn't know any better, I would have assumed you had always been a Villain from how you talked to Mason." Ren chuckled.

Jinx shrugged. "He was rude. I won't allow anyone to talk to me like that. Not anymore."

Ren looked out over the crowd that began to dance. "I like who you are becoming. It suits you."

"Why are you spoiling me?" She asked, a question since she had seen the tiara.

"How can you want more when I give you everything you want and then some." He said.

Jinx pursed her lips. "It sounds as if you're scared I'll leave."

"And if I am?" He asked, his head turning to her.

Jinx saw how the light caught in his eyes. "I would say you are very stupid."

He placed a hand on the column, leaning towards her. "Then I guess I am stupid."

Jinx felt her breath catch in her throat. She hated how he made her overthink everything in just seconds of getting close to her.

He suddenly pushed off the wall, taking her hand. "Let's dance, Dorian. I didn't take you to the most exclusive party to stand on the side."

She rolled her eyes, willingly following him to the dance floor. Jinx wondered if Villains had different dances from Heroes, though she doubted it. They all originated from the same place after all.

Ren spun her to face him, his hand immediately going around her waist. "Do you know how to waltz?"

Jinx scoffed. "You think that I don't after my mother trained me to be a Love Interest?"

Ren smirked, looking over her. "Let's see if you can keep up with me then."

Jinx loved the challenge, hoping he wasn't a lousy dancer himself.

Jinx placed her hand on his shoulder, her back straightening instinctively. The music started, a beautiful collection of notes she had never heard before. It was dark, but also seductive.

Ren stepped towards her, Jinx stepping back, moving to the side then it was her turn to step towards him.

"Good, you know the basics." He teased.

"You're starting to get on my nerves." She chuckled.

"Let's see how you do moving a bit faster."

They moved faster, Jinx following his movements expertly like they had been dancing together for years. He turned suddenly, Jinx smiling as she moved with him.

"There it is." Ren said.

Jinx furrowed her brows. "What?"

"My payment, a true smile." He gleamed.

Jinx rolled her eyes. "I have smiled a few times today; you haven't been paying attention obviously."

"Oh, I have seen those, but this is the first one to accompany a sparkle in your eyes." He said, looking at her with a softness.

"Careful, Ren, you are going to expose your adoration for me in public," Jinx teased, "You have to keep up appearances."

He spun her out, her arm extending before he moved closer to her again. "In Vileterra, they can see my weaknesses and still fear me. It just means I would kill to keep you, just as my father had."

Jinx snorted, tearing her eyes from him. "I am not worth the trouble; you'd be wasting your time."

"Jinx, you are worth more to me than you can ever imagine." He spoke with such sincerity it scared her. He couldn't possibly want someone like her, she was nothing but a burden to everyone in her life. Once he figured that out, he would toss her aside.

She didn't respond to his admission; she didn't know how to tell him the reasons he should toss her to the side. It was better for him to do it sooner rather than later. Jinx didn't want to be hurt again.

The song ended, and Jinx exited the floor. A Henchman passed with a tray of champagne, Jinx taking one and sipping on it. She cupped her hip, breathing in deeply.

"I am going to get us something stronger," Ren said, "I'll be right back."

Jinx nodded, watching as he disappeared into the crowd. She stood there, drinking down the rest of her champagne when she heard a voice behind her.

"You're the Dorian girl, right?"

Jinx turned seeing a large man dressed in a maroon suit. His eyes were a glowing red, the tips of his otherwise curly brown hair matching the color. From his nose came plumes of black smoke, Jinx trying her hardest not to cough from the assault to her senses.

"I'm Vince Killingly."

"Killingly?" Jinx scoffed, "Isn't that a bit on the nose for a Villain?"

He smiled, his teeth blackened and sharpened into jagged points. Immediately, Jinx became uncomfortable.

"I like to think of it as a weapon, everyone knows the Killingly name." He boasted proudly.

Jinx put a finger to her lip, pretending to think. "Yeah, no, I've never heard of it."

He was shocked, head jerking back. Vince smiled weakly. "You're just teasing me."

"No, I honestly never heard of your family name. Were you minor Villains?" Jinx knew she was getting under his skin but she couldn't help it. Teasing this man was an ego boost for herself.

Vince scoffed, opening his hand to reveal a ball of fire dancing across his palm. "Can a minor Villain do this?"

Jinx nodded. "Yes, that's basic magic."

She actually didn't know if it was, but assumed that Ren or his mother would most likely be able to produce a ball of flame like the one Vince was showing off.

Quicker than she had anticipated, Vince had his hand around her neck and threw her body against the wall so hard it caused cracks in the plaster. Everyone stopped, looking at Vince holding Jinx up. Her feet were a few inches off the ground, and she could feel the heat from his hand around her neck.

"Pathetic." Jinx spit, a menacing smile forming on her lips. "You have no idea what you just did."

Ren came up from behind Vince taking him by the jaw and throwing him into a column. His face softened as he looked to Jinx.

"Are you okay?" He asked.

She nodded, rubbing her neck. Ren removed her hand, exposing a red and light purple bruise that was beginning to form in the shape of a hand. Ren clenched his jaw, eyes darkening.

"Make him suffer." Jinx said, her own eyes giving a malicious glow.

Ren's head jerked to Vince who was stumbling after being thrown. As Ren approached him, Vince backed away, his hands raised.

"Don't do this in front of a crowd, Valder." Vince said warily.

"And why shouldn't I?" Ren spit. "Was it not obvious she was my claim, and yet you still chose to target her, thus targeting me."

"I didn't know." Vince sputtered. "I promise you I didn't."

Ren disappeared from his spot, appearing behind Vince. He grabbed the back of his neck throwing his face to the ground. The tiles splintered, large cracks extending outwards from the impact. Jinx gasped, not realizing how powerful Ren really was.

Vince quickly stood up, his nose shifted to the side unnaturally, a few of his sharpened black teeth chipped. Ren was on a path where he would not stop, Jinx could see it from the fury in his eyes. She knew the only one who could possibly stop him from ruining his image, would be herself.

She took several elegant steps forward, heels clicking against the tile floor loudly as everyone silently watched her. She kept her back straight and her head held high as she approached Ren, unfazed.

As she got to him, Jinx stepped into his eye view. He paused, gazing into her light gray eyes. She placed a hand on his chest, it was much firmer than she had expected, but she brushed the thought to the side.

"Don't waste your energy on him," She whispered, "He's not worth it."

Ren gritted his teeth looking between Jinx and Vince. "He should die for what he did to you."

Jinx smiled, it reaching her eyes. "As much as I adore your enthusiasm, I would become a target for other Villains to use you. That doesn't seem too fair to me."

Ren breathed out heavily, shaking his head. "A Villain would've let me kill him."

"But I'm not a Villain, I'm Morally Gray." Jinx smirked. "If you killed everyone who looks or touches me wrong, who would kill their Heroes?"

Ren tucked her hair behind her ears, kissing her forehead. Jinx paused, not expecting such an obvious sign of affection towards her. She knew her cheeks were a bright red from the heat that poured over her face.

He walked past her, towards Vince and squatted to where the Villain sat. "Next time, I won't let her stop me from killing you." He said it loudly enough for the others to hear. It wasn't just a warning for Vince, but for the others as well.

She couldn't help the sly smile that crossed her lips. Never in her life did Jinx think she would be attracted to someone threatening to kill another. Then, she saw Vince stand as Ren walked away.

"Oh, we're not done." Jinx said, facing Vince with her eyebrows raised. His eyes widened as she approached, backing into the same wall he had thrown her into. "You forget who I am."

Her fist punched through the plaster of the wall beside his face, her eyes sparkling at the fear it caused him.

"I-I'm sorry, Ms. Dorian." He sputtered.

"Not yet you aren't." She punched with her opposite hand, his head jerking to the side as he fell in a lump onto the floor.

Ren glided across the space between them, throwing a hand over her shoulders. He ushered her to the door, pausing to stop at a gaping mouthed Mason.

"Do you typically let ignorant Villains into your parties?" Ren snapped. "Obviously, this is not a hall of good repute anymore."

Mason closed his mouth, a finger flicking towards Vince. As they walked out, Jinx could hear Vince's loud objections and Henchmen tried to kick him out. She regretted not hitting him harder.

"You didn't have to do that." Jinx said

Ren rolled his eyes. "It was the smallest form of punishment he deserved. I wasn't the only one who did something either."

Jinx smirked. "I think the broken nose served him well enough, but it felt good to hit something."

He rubbed his jaw, shaking his head. "I might kill you, then we won't have this problem in the future."

"We both know you won't do that." Jinx said, placing her hand on his chest. "You're obsessed with me."

He placed his hand over hers, holding it there as they walked. "I hate when you're right."

"But Ren, darling, I'm always right." Jinx jabbed, wiggling her eyebrows. Ren smiled, softer than she had expected from him.

"Close your eyes, Dorian, I'm taking you home." Ren said.

"After the party had just begun, what a shame." She teased.

In one move he was carrying her and they were back in the cave he had first taken her to.

He set her down, smiling. "Funny, you didn't complain."

"You really didn't give me time to." She objected. "And you left our coats."

Ren shrugged. "Mason will send them to me tomorrow."

She looked away, sighing. She hated the way he was so nonchalant about everything.

"Thank you for the night out, but it's time for me to go to bed." She said, crossing her arms. She wanted him to protest, to steal her away somewhere.

"If that's what you want, I won't stop you." He said, closing the distance between them.

"Did you have something else in mind?" She asked.

He smirked, his hand reaching up and twirling in her hair. "I haven't shown you the gardens yet."

Jinx's mind went to the book of poisons, her heart skipping a beat. She had been meaning to go to the gardens, but she hadn't had time within the last few days.

"I'd love that." She gleamed.

He wrapped his arm around her waist, pulling her closer to him. Their bodies were pressed against each other in such an intimate manner that Jinx couldn't help but imagine what it would be like without clothes on.

"Hold on."

And with that, Ren teleported Jinx to the gardens.

Chapter Six
A Flower Ever So Deadly

Jinx had never realized how large the Valder Manor was until standing in the garden. It spanned longer than she had imagined it to, four towers peaking into the sky, one of which completely obscured by clouds. Around the entire property was a tall, gray, brick wall, a magical blue field extending up from where the physical wall stopped.

While the inside did not look like a Villain's lair, the outside did.

The garden, however, looked like something out of a fairytale. The moon shed light onto the glowing flowers and plants, flashing of lightning bugs dancing around them. There were normal flowers and plants mixed in with the glowing ones, but they were not as vibrant.

Ren grabbed Jinx's hand, holding it as he led her around.

"This is beautiful." She gasped, walking beneath an arch where bright pink flowers grazed her hair.

"It's one of the only things I like in Vileterra." Ren smiled. "I planted and cared for most of them myself."

Jinx looked to him, his face reflecting the blue glow of the upcoming *venenum flos*. He looked so peaceful when walking through, a different side to him that Jinx had yet to discover.

She looked towards the flowers she had read about, surprised at how beautiful they were. "This is *venenum flos*, I read about them in that book about poisons and magic."

She bent down towards the flowers looking closely at them. The blue glow was more intense than she had expected, though the tips of the flowers were red, as if dipped in blood. The were four sections to each petal, split off a single base. The stem was black with emerald green thorns. In the center, long tails of curled filaments pointed towards the sky.

"They have different ways to prepare them, you know." Jinx started, remembering what she had learned in her book. "One way is to boil them, it takes two petals for a person to go into a coma, four for a slow death, and six for a quick one."

"Then you can dry out the leaves and ground them into a powder to blow onto your victim, that's how Madam Vulcan killed her Hero, or bake them into a loaf of bread because it can taste just like cinnamon." Jinx paused. "Though, I'm not sure how the author found that out."

She looked up to Ren, smiling. He gazed at her in a way that made her heart stop. His green eyes glistening as he listened to her speak, complete and utter focus on each word she said.

"There is one other use of *venenum flos*," He said, "They don't tell it to you in the books."

Jinx furrowed her brows. "What is it?"

Ren knelt beside her, lightly touching a thorn on the side. "If you peel off four thorns, combine with basil, and lavender with just a drop of lemon juice, you will create a love potion."

Jinx smiled looking over the impressive plant. "Have you ever created it? A love potion?"

She wasn't sure she wanted to know the answer.

"No," He said, "The issue with the potion is that you need to lack love, it is meant for someone else to become your pawn."

Jinx bit her lip, it was not the romanticized idea of the love potion she expected. But if he never used it, does that mean he was in love with someone?

"Who are you in love with?" She blurted, not realizing those words would come out so straightforward.

He chuckled. "A girl we knew in school. She never noticed me, so the love was always one sided."

"I'm sorry." Jinx said. She knew how it felt to love a person without them reciprocating it. Her love for her parents had led to her heartache and eventual goal in life to become someone important.

"Don't worry your darling little head about it, Dorian. My father always said love finds a way." He said, lifting from the ground and offering her his hand.

She took it, walking along side him towards a large collection of thorned hedges. "Ren, what is that?"

He smirked. "A maze. Would you like to try and solve it?"

Jinx gleamed. She had never been in a maze before and the idea of a game always made her giddy. She was not allowed to play games with other kids growing up for fear that she would ruin her family's reputation by losing.

"Can we?" She asked, a sparkle in her eye.

"We can do whatever you want." Ren chuckled.

Jinx jogged to the maze entrance, the darkness within not causing her to become nervous due to the excitement she was experiencing. The twirling mass of thorns and black leaves were accompanied by a swirling fog that concealed the high heeled shoes she wore. With the heels digging into the dirt, she slipped them off, placing them beside the entrance.

"Would you like to make it a competition?" He asked with a sly smile.

"I have a feeling you will win, this is your maze after all." Jinx teased, though an uneasy feeling erupted in her stomach.

"Let's do this, I will refrain from using my power to teleport, and you will see what else you can do besides your magic blocking abilities." He smiled. "Two birds with one stone."

"And if I can't do anything except block magic?" She asked.

He nodded his head to the side. "If you don't make it to the center after an hour, I'll come find you."

"But no powers if you do." She laughed. "You have to do it the old-fashioned way."

His smiled dropped, looking at her with his eyes glowing.

"What?" She asked nervously.

"That's the first time you've actually laughed for me." He said lifting his hand to cup her cheek. "It was beautiful."

She smiled, pushing him away. "I get a head start, you already know this maze!"

Her stomach twisted as she went through the darkness, thinking over Ren's pleased expression at her laugh. Had it been so long since she had shown sincere pleasure in something? When was the last time she laughed? She couldn't remember.

Jinx got to her first choice, left, right, or straight. She looked to the right, seeing the hedge ending, blocking the path. To the left it went down, leading to another intersection, and straight led to a right turn. She assumed the maze wouldn't be too difficult, going straight and turning to the right. Dead end.

She turned back, only there were new options, the way she came closed off. She realized then that her choices needed to be sincere and carefully planned. She only had one shot to decide where she needed to go.

Turning back she had two options, right or left. She tried to picture the maze in her mind like one from an activity book. Instead of knowing all the information, she looked at it like she was discovering a new section as she moved over it. To the right she saw a few options all leading to a dead end. Opening her eyes, she went left. She continued the pattern, cursing as she ended up at a dead end. Then she heard Ren.

"Ten minutes and I'm coming to find you!"

Had it already almost been an hour? She shook her head, feeling the pressure well up inside of her. She could do this, it's nothing but a simple game.

Jinx closed her eyes focusing on the maze. She couldn't get a clear picture of it, only a small piece that she was in. She clenched her jaw breathing in deeply. She couldn't lose, if she lost bad things would happen. So she tried a different tactic.

She furrowed her brows, focusing on Ren. The map opened up inside her brain, and she walked, eyes closed as the images of where she was to go played for her like a movie.

There was a green glow to each turn that she was to take, each time the glow grew brighter as if knowing she was getting closer to him. Left, right, straight, straight, right, left, left, right. She followed the glow until she stopped seeing the movie in her mind and only saw black.

Jinx opened her eyes, her mouth dropping open as she looked over the center of the maze. The fog was gone, clearly showing baby blue grass beneath her feet. A path of large smooth stones led from where she stood to a fountain. The fountain was black, a figure frozen as he fell back, his hands over his throat where red water escaped. More flowers surrounded the perimeter, various benches placed expertly. By the fountain, Ren stood, his body glowing a brilliant green of his power.

"Don't come too close, I don't know what is happening with my magic." He warned.

Jinx ignored him, smiling. "I think it was me."

"What do you mean?" He asked, a worried frown on his face.

She walked towards him, her fingers playing through the magic that swirled around her hands like smoke.

"When I was making my way through the maze, I was trying to picture what it looked like. It helped some, but then you told me I only had ten minutes left, so I focused on you instead." She admitted, staring at his green aura. "There was a green light that I see around you sometimes, it showed me where to go, which way to turn, each time getting brighter as I got closer to you."

"That's around the same time my magic went haywire." He muttered, gazing at her.

"But it led me here, and I didn't lose." She gleamed.

He placed a hand on her arm, the magic light around him disappearing. He laughed as he saw it go, smiling brightly.

"Magic resistance and magic detection. What a duo." He said proudly. "With some training, you could be unstoppable."

"How?" She asked, shaking her head.

"Everyone has some sort of magic as a Hero or Villain, even some Love Interests or Best Friends. With you being able to detect that, and possibly identify the types of magic, you could warn others before it's used."

"Almost like an oracle of power?" She asked.

"Exactly." He beamed.

"Huh, if only my father could see me now." She said sarcastically.

Ren shook his head, grabbing her chin. "He will not see you until you can use your magic. I forbid it."

Jinx lifted her brows. "I do love when you get all protective over me, as if you have any control."

There was an intense sparkle in his eyes that was combined with one side of his lips twisted upwards. "I have more control over you than you believe, Dorian, do not tempt me into showing you."

She bit her lip at the challenge, her eyes grazing slowly over his body. As much as she hated Love Interest training, it did give her some things that were useful. Her hand pushed away his, it falling easily from her chin, her fingers wrapping around his throat. She felt a surge of power as she did the movement, a vicious smile crossing her lips.

"Kneel." She ordered.

He scoffed. "I don't take orders from you-."

Jinx pressed a pressure point on his neck, his knees collapsing from the pain. "Good boy."

Ren shook his head, licking his teeth. "Do you even know who I am?"

Jinx looked at him sideways. "Nothing more than a Henchman to me."

Ren pulled at her hand, throwing out a leg so that she fell. His arm caught her before her body hit the ground, letting her land softly in the blue grass. She cursed this dress he had picked for her, not giving her the proper room to use her legs.

"My dear Dorian, did you honestly think I would let you best me, in my own garden at that?" Ren hissed playfully.

"We both know you love when I get the upper hand on you, don't you dare deny it." Jinx whispered, trying to make her voice as seductive as possible. Something she was never good at.

He leaned his head down, their faces inches apart. His finger traced down her face leaving a tickling sensation after it. "If only you knew the things that go through my head when I look at you."

"Torture, murder, the occasional anger that my poor vases are subjected to." Jinx teased. "The knowledge that I could kill or accompany you depending on the side I choose."

He wiggled his eyebrows. "What a prospect. Jinx Dorian, a Villain with no rival."

"Threat to all and friend to none." She whispered.

"How dastardly evil." He breathed.

Jinx smiled. "A better Villain than you?"

Ren scoffed. "No one can be better than me, but you will possibly become my equal."

"I like the sound of that. A Queen of Villains, equal to Ren Valder."

Ren smirked. "You know what I told you about using my family name."

She reached her hand up his chest. "Valder." She said slowly, pronouncing each syllable.

"You're a cruel woman, Dorian."

"Only for you."

He moved his head lower, his lips brushing down her ear. "Tell me to stop and I will." His lips touched beside her earrings that he had given her earlier that night. She gasped, but moved her head for better access.

She had never been touched like this.

His knee found it's way between her thighs, locking her legs into the already tight dress. His hand cradled her neck, fingers pressing into the skin. It hurt, but she enjoyed the sting that accompanied it. Ren's lips grazed down her neck, Jinx's breathing getting heavier as he continued. He stopped at her collarbone, his teeth prodding the flesh. Her hand went to his hair, holding his head down to her.

Whatever he was doing, it ignited a fire within her, heat encompassing her body.

His head moved back to her ear as he whispered, "I told you I have control over you, Dorian. Just look how your body begs for me."

She stalled, unsure of how to respond.

He pulled away.

Jinx felt the flash of disappointment run through her, dancing along the fire held inside her body. He stood, offering her a hand to stand with him. She didn't look at him as she took it, his actions torturous to her.

She should have known he would not continue, after all he already admitted to loving someone else. Them being together was taboo, a daughter of a Hero, no matter how disgraced from her family, and a Villain, did not belong together.

Even so, Jinx was disappointed. As much as she hated to admit it, she wanted Ren to want her the way he wanted that girl he loved. She was claimed by him, sure, but how long would he stay? She was interesting right now, Morally Gray with powers to detect and block magic. But when his interest fades, would she just be another person living in his home? Is it possible that Ren would abandon her like the rest of the world had?

A warm hand caressed her cheek, Ren looking at her.

"I am respecting your boundaries, if I did not stop then, I would've never stopped." He said quietly.

Jinx nodded, her hands fiddling in front of her, eyes fixated on them. Did she do something wrong? Is it possible she was not fit for someone to see her as a Love Interest, even if she was Morally Gray?

"Let's get you to bed." Ren said, picking her up and cradling her in his arms. She didn't complain as he took her, resting her head against his chest and hand playing with the buttons on his suit.

He did not teleport them to the cave, but to the library of her tower. She waited for him to lower her, but he didn't, instead carrying her up to her room.

"You don't have to keep carrying me." She objected, though she didn't fight it. If she was being honest with herself, she liked it.

"I want to, at least give me that." He smiled weakly.

He opened the door to her bedroom, letting her down softly. She walked to her bed, pulling the PJ's from beneath her pillow.

"Close the door, but don't leave yet please?" She said weakly.

He nodded, closing the door to let her change.

She let the dress drop off her body, throwing on the gray t-shirt that was three sizes too big and the plaid shorts. She opened the door, walking down the steps to stop at the overly large closet, removing the crown and earrings and placing them into the case. They were easily the largest and possibly most expensive items in her growing collection.

Once removing her makeup and putting her hair into a long braid at her side, she went down to the library. Nerves rolled in her stomach, wondering if Ren actually waited for her. As he promised, Ren stood hands behind his back looking out the window towards the garden.

She didn't know what she was going to say to him, she had just wanted him to stay. Jinx was never going to amount more to him than a plaything, someone to distract him from the love he could never have, but she still wanted him.

He looked up to her, his mouth dropping and eyes widening.

She cursed herself, remembering he had never seen her dressed down. "I'm sorry, I will go put something else on-."

"No, you will not." He said, his hand wrapping around hers. Did he teleport to get to her quicker? "Every day you show me how beautiful you are." He muttered, Jinx assuming she misheard him.

"What?"

"Nothing," He smiled, "What can I do for you before you go to bed?"

"Who are you in love with?" Jinx blurted. "I-I'm only asking because I might've known her." She hated how nervous the question sounded.

"You do know her, and I will not be telling you, not yet." He winked. "Some information for you to look forward to."

Jinx nodded, opening, and closing her mouth, but no other words came out. "I'm just going to read a bit before bed, Ren. You can go if you'd like."

Ren nodded, looking Jinx over one last time before making his way to the door.

Jinx watched him leave, sitting down onto the stairs and running her hands through her hair. She sighed deeply, hating herself for having those rolling feelings of anxiety within her. She barely knew Ren, but everything he did for her was all she had ever wanted in life; all she had ever wanted in a partner. She should've known she would never be so lucky to find love like this, after all, who could love someone who was neither good nor evil.

She stood, making her way up the stairs. The roaring lion handle mocked her as she made her way into the room.

"You're an idiot, Jinx, a whole idiot."

Chapter Seven
The Act of Heroes and Villains

Over the few weeks that Jinx had been at Valder Manor, she began to get used to Ren being around. Even if they were not specifically doing things together, she had found his company pleasurable.

They had fallen into a pattern. Jinx would wake up, Ren waiting for her in the library below her room. He would always have a coffee waiting, made to her exact specifications, even better than the coffee from Central City. After a few hours of talking and reading, he would walk with her to the kitchen, making a meal way too extravagant for a simple breakfast and they would eat together. He always made sure she ate her fill, then they would take a walk. He claimed it was good for digestion, though she was pretty sure he liked being in the gardens. They would do some sparring after, Ren having yet to beat her in a duel. Then there was lunch, some relaxation time, and for dinner he either made plans for restaurants or cooked for her again.

Jinx loved their daily lives, growing fonder of Ren each day. She had taught herself a bit of magic, nothing too exciting, a simple fire that would light on her fingertip, a spell that reduced frizz from her hair, and a way for her to make items invisible as long as they were able to fit into her palm.

She was proud of her progress and used those few spells to tease Ren. Jinx was able to smile freely and did not feel as stressed anymore. Life was easy, but when she woke up that morning, Ren was not waiting in the library with her coffee. Immediately, she felt a knot in her stomach.

Throwing on a sweater and leggings, Jinx went to the kitchen. Maybe he was just running a bit late and making her coffee?

As she opened the double door to the kitchen, she was surprised that it was not Ren within, but his mother.

"Good morning, Jinx." She said, smiling at her. "Would you like some breakfast?"

"Morning, no breakfast for me. Do you know where Ren is?" She was nervous being around Cosmic Sorceress alone.

"Oh, he went to Central City. Micha was practically calling Ren to fight him." She said casually. "Would you like to see?"

Jinx nodded and Cosmic Sorceress opened a door to reveal a television inside. She turned it on, it showing Micha on the sorting stage.

"Jinx Dorian is a threat to all, Honorville and Central City needs to be aware of the danger she poses." Micha said into a microphone.

Jinx furrowed her brows. "He said nothing about Ren."

Cosmic Sorceress smirked. "Darling, he insulted you. It is only natural that Ren defends your honor, if he didn't what a poor Villain he would be."

Jinx scoffed. "Isn't that a Hero thing? Defending the honor of another?"

Cosmic Sorceress gave her a side glance, her green eyes sparkling. "You know, Villains do not have a counterpart. They have Henchmen, sure, but they do not get Love Interests or Best Friends like Heroes do." She put her finger into the pot she had been stirring, making a face. "When a Villain finds their reason for their crimes, that's when the real battles begin."

"Are you saying Ren had found his passion?" She asked.

"Mmhmm." Cosmic Sorceress poured a cup of coffee into a mug, passing it to her along with the creamer and sugar. "My son has a passion like his father, driven by an obsession."

Jinx saw a beautiful smile cross her face, one that was unmistakably attached to a memory.

"Doesn't that cloud his judgement?" Jinx asked, concern flooding into her.

Cosmic Sorceress nodded. "It's a small price to pay on either side. I killed my nemesis easily, but I did not have a weakness."

"A weakness?" Jinx was confused.

"Every Villain has a weakness, Jinx, sometimes it comes quickly, other times after an event that changes the Villain's life." She took the pot off the burner, turning to her. "Let him fight for you, it's only in his nature."

Jinx looked back to the television seeing Ren with his masquerade mask on, fighting Micha. Micha punched him in the stomach sending Ren flying into a brick wall, the stones crumbling on top of him.

Jinx jumped from her seat, her hand to her mouth. "I-I need to help him."

Cosmic Sorceress shook her head. "You'd be more of a target than he is right now. All Heroes are after you, not just your other half."

Jinx watched as Ren appeared behind Micha, smiling maliciously as he pulled out a knife. Micha used the same move she had on him, throwing him to the ground and stabbing down. Ren dodged the blade, wrapping his legs around Micha and strangling him with his arm.

As Jinx looked at every movement Ren made, she couldn't help but feel a bit heated. No one had ever fought for her before. Not like Ren was. He looked as if Micha had killed her, his eyes crazed, teeth showing like a raging dog.

She sat in the chair, hands in her lap. It was all for her. The cooking, coffee, spending time with her, making sure she ate, hot baths every night. He did that all for her.

"Ren said you are starting to learn a bit of magic?" Cosmic Sorceress asked snapping Jinx out of her trance.

"Yeah, I learned a few things, but nothing too impressive." She said.

"If you would like, I could teach you more. It has been a while since I had a student." She looked Jinx up and down. "Show me what you've learned so far."

Jinx contorted her hand, running the other one over it. When it lifted off, her finger lit with a green flame.

"Good, what else?"

She grabbed a napkin, holding it in her palm and willing the napkin to disappear. Opening her hand, she could not see the napkin anymore, but felt it still there.

Cosmic Sorceress' eyes lit up. "That was one of my first spells. How cute!"

"The last one is only to make my hair less frizzy." Jinx admitted.

She chuckled. "I use that one every day." She shoved a spoonful of a gritty textured slop into her mouth. "I will lend you some books for beginner magic. I'll help you when you need, but if you were able to do basic spells like that you will have no problems."

Jinx smiled. "I'd appreciate that."

"I forgot to mention on our first meeting, you can call me mother or Meg. You will be spending quite a bit of time with us so formalities are left behind." She said. "You can call my husband, Knox."

Jinx nodded, though she knew it would take a while to think of them by their real names and not their Villain names.

Meg cringed, her eyes to the television. Jinx looked, seeing Ren with a large cut to his side. She clenched her jaw, nails digging into the palm of her hands. Blood escaped the small cuts she made, her breathing becoming shallow.

"I am going to go get the medical kit, he will need it." Meg mentioned, walking from the kitchen.

Jinx couldn't move as she stared at the tv, anxiety building in her throat. She hated that she was so upset over watching him get hurt, a few weeks ago she barely thought twice about him.

Ren produced a ball of light in his hand, thrusting it forward and hitting Micha with it. Micha immediately laid unconscious, Ren looking to the camera that recorded the fight.

"Ms. Dorian is under my protection, do not talk ill of her unless you want to die."

Jinx felt her heartbeat in her chest, her head swirling. He just announced that to the entirety of not only Central City but Honorville and Vileterra as well.

He disappeared from the screen, Jinx knowing that he was coming back.

She leaped from her seat, running to the cave where he always teleported into. He had explained how his mother had created it so he would not be followed, a habit for him to enter through it now.

He was already in the hall when she got to that end of the manor.

"Ren." She whispered, stopping in her tracks.

He looked up, smiling to her. "Good morning, Dorian, sorry I didn't bring you your coffee."

She rushed to him, throwing her arms around his neck, squeezing him tightly. He could've died and without telling her goodbye. She hated him for that, but for some reason, Jinx was so happy he was alright.

"If I would've known I would be greeted like this after a fight, I would've done it sooner."

"Shut up you fool." She whispered.

"As much as I want you to continue holding me like this, I do need to stitch up my side." He chuckled.

Jinx jumped back, looking at the bleeding wound he had from Micha's stab. "Fuck, Ren."

She rushed him towards the kitchen, Meg there with a black bag of supplies.

"Take off your shirt." Jinx ordered, Ren smiling as he removed his suit jacket, then button down shirt. She removed his black and white mask, placing it on the counter.

She pulled out gauze from the bag, Meg watching with raised eyebrows. Jinx shook her head, looking to Ren through her lashes.

"You're lucky I don't kill you for this." She spit.

He smirked. "Always with the sudden switch in your feelings towards me."

"You could've been killed," She scolded, "A touch to the right and he would've hit your liver."

"But he didn't." Ren teased.

"Jinx, how do you know so much about healing?" Meg asked.

"She wanted to be a doctor before the sorting." Ren answered for her. "Who would've known it would come in handy."

"I shouldn't have to use it in the first place." Jinx grumbled.

Meg smiled, walking to the door. "I will leave you to it, looks like you have it covered."

There was silence between them when Meg left, Jinx stitching up Ren's wounds, enjoying the flinching. When she was finished, she assessed her work, eyes glazing over his chest and stomach. Her breath caught in her throat, not realizing the perfection of his muscles.

"Like what you see?" Ren smirked, leaning back to expose them to her. "You can touch them if you want."

Jinx narrowed her eyes at him. "I am not going to do that, there's too much gratification for you."

"Don't be like that, Dorian." He teased.

"I'm mad at you, Ren. Don't think a simple show of your muscles could change that." She snapped.

He huffed. "What on earth could you be mad at me for?"

"Figure it out." She snarled walking to the door.

His hand caught her wrist, her head snapping back to him. He looked to her exposed palm, seeing the small cuts she had created on them with her nails. His face darkened as he looked to them, eyes flicking up to her.

"How did this happen." He growled.

She tugged her arm back, but he held it tightly. She scrunched up her face angrily, clenching her jaw. "You left. You left without telling me goodbye or where you were going." She yelled. "I had to watch you get thrown into buildings and stabbed on television. How do you think that made me feel?" His eyes widened, head jerking back. "We have a routine. I look forward to that routine every day." She said with tears in her eyes. "What happens if one day you leave to fight Micha and he kills you? There's no more routine after that."

Jinx ripped her hand from him, huffing. "You can't take yourself away from me. You're the only person who truly cares."

He marched towards her, closing their distance, his hand cupping her cheek. He pressed his forehead to hers, her thumbs latching onto the belt loops of his pants.

"I am so sorry," He whispered, "I didn't know how much this would hurt you."

"You could've died." Her voice cracked.

He shook his head against hers. "I wouldn't leave you like that."

"How can I trust you?" She said quietly.

Ren grabbed her hand. "Come on."

He pulled her down halls, ruffly turning corners, Jinx having a hard time keeping up.

"Ren, where are we going?"

His hand tightened around her wrist as he opened a black door and thrust her inside.

The room was large, weapons stacked neatly on the wall, next to an iron bedframe. The bed was a mess, not having been made since its occupant left. The floor was the same stone tiles that the library below her room had, no rug covering the cold surface. A wardrobe stood in the corner; a door propped open so Jinx could see the black suits that she constantly saw Ren in, occupying the inside.

Ren slammed the door shut, going to a desk across from his bed. He opened the drawers, pouring papers onto the once cleaned surface.

"Every Villain has a weakness to them, Dorian. No matter how hard they try to hide it, to the outside it's obvious." Ren said piling more papers and pictures onto the wooden surface. "For my father, it was my mother. He obsessed over her, fixated on her to a point where he didn't care about defeating his Hero, only protecting her."

Jinx was confused, what did this have to do with her?

"My mother's weakness was me. It was how she was able to kill Spectra, her Hero, so easily. Until I was born, she didn't have any weakness."

Jinx nodded, biting her lip. That was what Meg had told her that morning.

"Unfortunately for me, I took after my father." He waved his hand to the desk, willing her to look at the display over it. She was shocked, seeing pictures of her from back in school up until a day before the robbery. She never was looking directly into the camera in those pictures, always focusing on someone else.

Along with the pictures, there were papers. She picked one up, realizing it was a report card. Her report card. She looked through a notebook, pages lined with a play by play of her day, some dating back to her first days in school.

Ren had been watching her.

Her mouth dropped open, fear flooding into her as she read page after page of content about her. It was all about her.

"You've been stalking me?"

"I couldn't help it. You're my weakness, Dorian. Even before the sorting I knew I was a Villain due to this." He motioned at the papers. "I tried to stop, but as soon as I saw you again, it was an impulse I couldn't control."

Jinx peddled back, sitting on the end of the bed. "Did you-did you watch me change?"

Ren's eyes widened. "I may be a stalker, but I'm not a pervert."

Jinx nodded, looking to a picture of her smiling next to some former friends. "And my-my sorting didn't change your opinion of me?"

Ren walked towards Jinx, kneeling before her. "Nothing in this world, and I mean nothing, could make me not want you, Jinx."

Jinx looked to him, surprised to hear her name come from his lips. "I should be scared of you."

He nodded. "You should."

"I should want to run away, to escape because this," She motioned to the desk. "This is not normal, Ren."

His jaw tightened. "Then why don't you?"

Jinx shook her head, looking away from him. "I-I don't know."

His hand reached up, cupping her cheek, and gently forcing her to look at him. "I won't hurt you."

She nodded, a tear slipping down her cheek. "I know, but if I'm your weakness, they could use me to hurt you." She shuttered. "What if I get attached to you? What if I get used to having you around and then you die?"

Jinx already knew she was attached to him. If something like that morning happened again, she wouldn't know what to do.

She couldn't hold back the tears that fell, sucking in a painful gasp. Ren stood quickly, wrapping his arms around her. Jinx clung to him, his arms so strong as he held her.

"I won't leave you, Jinx Dorian. I won't ever hurt you in that way." He kissed the top of her head as she sobbed into his chest. "I would burn the world down to keep you safe and will kill anyone who stands between us."

"Promise?" She asked weakly.

"Jinx, I'd promise you it to you if it would make you smile just for a second."

Jinx gasped lifting her head to look at him, Ren brushing away her tears.

"I can't give you anything back." She whispered.

Ren smiled softly, his hand cupping the back of her neck. "My dear, you being here with me is all I could want."

She placed a shaking hand to his, intertwining her fingers into it. "Ren," She said nervously. "The girl you love, from school, is she-."

"You." He said without a pause. "Jinx Dorian, it has always been you."

Her hands wrapped around his neck, pulling his face to hers. She pressed her lips to his, Ren not hesitating as he accepted the kiss.

"If you leave me, I will kill you." She promised as her lips parted from his.

"If I leave you, I will hand you the dagger to kill me."

She looked to him, a man who was supposed to be her complete opposite. Someone who grew up on the idea of Villains and hate while she grew up on perfection and Heroism. Somehow, in the grand scheme of things, Ren Valder had found and saved her. Against all odds, Jinx had found comfort in a killer.

"Ren," She said quietly, for his ears alone. "I am yours."

He let a cocky smile loose on his lips. His hand went up, brushing away stray pieces of her hair. "Of course, you are. You had no choice but to be." He moved his face closer to hers. "As much as you would've tried to fight it, I always get what I want."

And that was it. Jinx Dorian, daughter of a notorious Hero, accepted Ren Valder, a notorious Villain's claim. No matter what happened, Jinx was his and his alone.

Chapter Eight
A Broken Treaty

Ren had refused to leave Jinx's side all day. They did not follow their routine, relaxing in each other's company. There never came a point when Ren was not touching her in some way or doing something to please her. Even when cooking, Ren had propped Jinx on the counter, talking with her like they had known each other for years. Which, in Ren's case, he had.

"I'm going to get fat if you keep feeding me like this." Jinx teased as she licked the beater he had offered her.

"I like to garden, and I like to cook. Now I have someone to cook and garden for." He smirked.

Jinx grinned. "If I hadn't known the types of plants in your garden, I would've been skeptical that you were really a Villain."

"Villains are allowed to have hobbies, Dorian, mine are just less conventional."

The news broke through on the television, an emergency report. "This just in, the treaty between Heroes and Villains was broken-." Ren paused, his body tensing. "Hero Thaddeus Dorian, son of Packard Dorian, spotted in the Vileterra Mountain range. All citizens of Honorville and Central City be on alert as Villains now have free reign!"

Jinx stared at the screen, her brother's smiling face pictured in the corner.

"Who is your brother's Villain?" Ren's voice was tight, his knuckles white against the spoon.

Jinx shook her head. "He wasn't assigned one, it claimed not identified on his sorting."

"Fuck." Ren shoved the pot off the burner, flicked off the stove and grabbed Jinx. She slid off the counter dropping the beater and stumbled as she was pulled behind Ren.

"What's going on?" She asked.

"Your brother is coming for you." He growled.

Jinx scoffed. "No he isn't, he's been on a quest, there's no way he would've known-."

Ren stopped, looking to her. "Those mountains are only miles away from the manor. Your brother is reported by those mountains, so what do you think would be his reason?"

Jinx furrowed her brows, shaking her head. "I-I don't want him to take me."

"And he won't." Ren promised, pulling her towards her room. "We need to pack."

"But where-." Jinx stopped, looking around her as she realized they were not in the hall, but her closet. "You could teleport me like this the entire time?"

Ren smirked, looking to her. "Of course I could."

Jinx clicked her tongue. "And you chose to make me cling to you?"

"I liked the way you hung on me."

"You're a nightmare." She huffed, walking next to him to pack her bags.

"Aw, my dear, that's the nicest thing you've ever said to me." Ren laughed, causing a smile to force its way upon her lips.

"Stop making me smile, we're supposed to be serious." She scolded, peaking to him.

He chuckled. "No promises. An unhinged woman always makes the people cower." Ren suddenly turned his head to the side as if hearing something. "He's already here. Forget the bags, let's go."

"How do you know?" Jinx asked, running and wrapping her arms around him.

He brought them to the center of the maze, the blue grass now turned a blood red, the walking path stones black. "The magical border is attached to my family's power. We all know who comes and goes."

"But they-."

"Already left, my father won't let my mother get hurt, remember? Same goes for me." He growled.

"Ren, I know my brother, he's just confused," Jinx said, "He won't hurt us."

He grabbed her face, forcing her to look at him. "I will not risk losing you, Jinx."

"Then let me fight with you," She begged, clutching the jacket of his suit. "I was trained as well as my brother, I know his flaws. You aren't matched to him, but I am." Ren shook his head, his jaw tightening. "Ren, please, I don't want to be useless."

"Don't make me regret this, Dorian. I will kill everyone if I lose you." He growled.

She smiled, going to her toes to kiss his cheek. "Don't tempt me with a good time."

He grabbed the back of her neck, forcing his lips to hers. She melted in his embrace, everything going away except for them. He pulled back, placing his forehead against Jinx's.

"You terrify me." He whispered.

"I need a weapon of some sort; my brother will be armed." She said, fear overpowering her. From their training, Jinx knew her brother would do what he could to save her, she is the damsel in distress. He did not have a Love Interest or Best Friend due to the fact he also did not have a nemesis. To Thaddeus, Jinx was the only thing that mattered.

"What do you want?" Ren asked.

Jinx shook her head. "A blade of some sort, preferably my dagger."

Ren hissed, his entire being rejecting the idea of leaving her. "Stay here. I will be back in a minute."

Jinx nodded. She waited until he was gone, pulling out the dagger he had given her. She didn't want him there when she faced her brother, he would only get in the way.

She closed her eyes, focusing on Thaddeus. There was a strange shimmering that she could see coming from the wall beyond the maze. She turned, watching the beacon of light as it pinpointed Thaddeus' path he made towards her. Opening her eyes, she watched as his sword cut through the leaves of the maze.

He looked awful, face covered in dirt, lines of sweat streaking down it. His body armor was equally as disgusting, twigs from the maze hedges stuck into it. His blond hair was turned an ashy white, hands covered in charcoal.

"Jinny, is that you?" He asked, a soft smile over his face. Guilt rolled through Jinx as she nodded, her knuckles turning white as she held the dagger behind her back. "I didn't mean to leave you here so long, there was a quest and I tried to make you a Hero, but it all went wrong-."

Jinx jerked her head back narrowing her eyes. "What do you mean you tried to make me a Hero?"

"The quest I told you about before I left. I could change the world with the dial, I tried to change your sorting, only there was not enough of your hair-."

"My hair?"

"Yes, for the dial to read who was supposed to be changed. Then I heard you were sorted Morally Gray and kidnapped by dad's nemesis-."

Jinx couldn't believe what she was hearing. This entire time, she thought the sorting had gone wrong, that her Morally Gray decision had been the right one. The Heroes and people of Central City trying to attack her was Thaddeus' fault. The entire reason she is a most wanted person is because Thaddeus fucked up.

"I was perfectly content being a BC, Thaddeus," She snapped, her eyes blazing in hatred. "I was happy living life in my normal routine, doing whatever the hell I wanted without eyes on me constantly." She sucked in a hissing breath. "I was no longer looked at by our parents, no longer targeted by Villains, my only job was to open a safe and do whatever else was needed of me." Jinx raised an arm, twisting her head to the side, trying to control her anger. "*You* were the one upset at my insignificant life, the one who was not beaten or ever wrong when we were kids." She threw her hand down, eyes fixated on him. "I was ruined by our parents and you did nothing!"

His face dropped, brows furrowing sadly. "I couldn't-."

"No, you could've! Some fucking Hero you became when you couldn't even protect your own fucking sister." Jinx yelled. "I *needed* you to protect me, to save me from them, but you never did. You know who did though? Ren Valder." Thaddeus shook his head as if he had heard her wrong. "Ren Valder saved me from our parents and all Central City when you failed me once again. He was the one who came and wanted to kill our father when he had seen the fucking scars over my back. He succeeded where you failed."

"He's a Villain, Jinn-."

"My name is Jinx!" She screamed. "Jinny died when you failed that quest and put a target on my back."

He placed his hand to his head, brushing back his dirty hair. "I don't understand, you were always so happy."

"I was miserable. My entire world was faked, and I had to pretend to be someone I never was." She laughed manically. "I hate bright colors and salads and fucking poetry. I like darkness and deadly poisons and the way that it feels to hold a knife to a person's throat." She looked down, smiling menacingly. Her eyes flashed up, her head not moving. "You created a god damned Villain."

"No," Thaddeus said, "No, he had brainwashed you into thinking that, Jinx you're a Hero."

"I'm not, Thad, I'm Morally Gray."

She rushed to him, her knife out from behind her back. Slamming it down, he blocked her attack, spinning her arm to try and pin her. She kicked out his feet, his grip loosening from her. Jinx tried to stab down on him again, his body twisting away from her. She jumped over him, rolling and twisting. He pulled his own, arching up to hit her. Jinx rammed her elbow into his head, grabbing his arm and twisting around it. She dug the arch of her foot under his chin, pressing at his artery. Only forty-eight seconds for Thaddeus to lose consciousness. She just needed to hold him there for forty-eight seconds.

"Jinx!" Ren called out to her.

She looked up, Thaddeus taking the opportunity to toss his knife and cut across the back of her knee. She felt a popping, her kneecap moving out of place. Jinx screamed out, Thaddeus throwing her off him and rising to a standing position. He snarled at Ren who's green eyes darkened and the light of his magic expanding around him. Thaddeus pulled a sword, Ren narrowing his eyes at him as he approached.

Jinx looked down to her knee, her brother had severed her tendon. There was no way she would be able to run or even walk to stop him. She looked to her side; her dagger was just out of reach.

She took in a large breath, watching as Ren and Thaddeus faced off. Ren held himself nicely, his body and feet placed perfectly with his eyes screaming revenge. Even without a weapon, Ren dodged and moved against Thaddeus' attacks as if he did have one.

Her body shook with the pain that radiated down her leg and into her hip. Jinx blew out an angry breath, grunting as she lifted herself onto her hands and uninjured leg, crawling slowly to the dagger.

Just as Ren refused to let her die, Jinx would do anything or kill anyone to keep him safe. Gritting her teeth, she grabbed the hilt of the dagger. She could stop all of this with one carefully aimed throw.

A boot stomped onto her extended arm, causing her to scream. Both Ren and Thaddeus stopped, looking at the man who had no sympathies when hurting his daughter. Packard Dorian. He sneered at her, twisting his boot, Jinx crying out as she felt a snapping.

"I raised you better than to try and murder your brother." He hissed.

"Fuck you." Jinx cried trying to push his boot off her arm. He pressed down harder, pain shooting through her whole body.

"For you to end up with a Villain, especially the son of my nemesis, what a fucking disgrace."

Jinx sobbed, pushing against the pain to grab the dagger. Her dagger that Ren had gifted her.

Packard picked it up before her, Jinx slinking back in defeat.

"This is the ugliest weapon I had ever seen." He said with a disgruntled tone. He tossed the dagger into the fountain, too far for Jinx to attempt to grab it.

She sobbed, dropping her head into her arm. She should've let Ren kill him before, this would've never happened if she had let him. Her whole plan was supposed to be like this, but now, Ren is against two Heroes. Two Heroes he was not matched with and could kill him because of her.

She watched his jaw tighten as her dad approached him, Thaddeus snarling as their dad got nearer.

"I wonder how my old friend Knox will feel with his son dying by my hand." Packard grinned. "Maybe he will finally come out of hiding."

Ren gritted his teeth looking past Packard to Jinx. She shook her head to him, she prayed he wouldn't do anything stupid. If her father killed Ren, there would be no stopping her. She would kill her father without hesitation. Ren was all she had left to lose.

"Thaddeus take your traitor sister home." Packard said patting him on the cheek. Jinx saw how Thaddeus' power brightened before he nodded and walked towards her.

Jinx looked to the flower beds she was next to, quickly attempting to run from him. Thaddeus grabbed her with ease, careful to tuck her broken arm over her chest.

"I'm sorry, Jinny." He said quietly.

"If he hurts Ren, I will never forgive you." She hissed.

Thaddeus looked to their father and Ren, sighing. "Dad, we got Jinx, just knock him out and leave him."

And that's exactly what Packard did. He swung his fist as Ren looked up to Jinx, the impact sending Ren flying into the hedges, the brick wall along the perimeter crumbling. Her chin shook and tears welled in her eyes as she prayed he was okay.

Thaddeus jogged, jumping into the air and took off flying, their father doing the same behind them.

"When did you learn to fly?" Jinx asked bitterly.

"It's not my power, it's dad's. I can absorb powers of others by being close enough or from their touch." Thaddeus said hollowly.

That explained the colorless aura around him, he had no power of his own, only a replicant of others. Jinx kept her head down as she focused on her ability to block power, envisioning a bubble around herself. When confident that Thaddeus would not sense her magic, Jinx closed her eyes, clutching the *venenum flos* petals in her hand. When she opened her eyes, she cracked open her fingers, the petals invisible.

She smiled, a new plan forming in her head. Jinx had chosen a side of good or evil, and if they called her a Villain, so be it.

Chapter Nine
Healing and Torture

Jinx was brought to a cabin in Honorville, one she had never been to before. It had been secluded into a forest, not accessible by foot. A red glowing barrier was placed in a dome around the building, it licking at Jinx as she passed through. It was a strange feeling, but she couldn't help the familiarity about it.

Thaddeus landed in a clearing before the front of the cabin, the group met by none other than Micha, standing in the doorway.

"Did you kill him?" Micha asked, looking at Jinx's bloody and bruised form.

"No, that's your job." Packard said, walking past him and patting him on the shoulder. Micha nodded, Thaddeus following him inside.

The cabin was nothing nice. It had one bed in the corner, brown and maroon stains over the uncovered mattress. There were iron chains connected to the metal bedframe, the shackles having a collection of dried red coating that Jinx knew wasn't rust. There was a metal pail beside the bed that Jinx hoped was not for what she thought. There was a single fireplace on the opposite side of the room, a simple wooden table with bench seats along the sides. There were a stack of blankets, canned food, and papers piled on top of the table, along with a large trunk on the floor at the end.

Jinx realized then, this was not a secluded get away cabin, but used to torture Villains and their Henchmen. Micha was here meaning he wanted information about Ren, something she would not give up so easily. She began to mentally prepare herself, pain was soon to come.

A plume of smoke shot up from the fire, a woman with a medical bag walking into the cabin. "This better be good, Packard."

Jinx recognized her, she was her dad's Best Friend, Jackie.

Packard's face contorted into one filled with sorrow and grief as he looked to her. "My daughter," He whimpered, "That son of a bitch hurt my daughter."

Jackie looked to Jinx who was still in Thaddeus' arms with a look of horror. She rushed to her, looking over her body, shaking her head.

"You're lucky I have healing magic, Pack, this is bad." She said, biting her lip. "Put her on the bed." Thaddeus did as she asked. She cried out as they tried to straighten out her leg, Jackie focusing on her severed tendon first. "I am so sorry you're hurting, Jinx, I'm going to make you better, okay?"

Jinx nodded, tears coming to her eyes from the woman's kindness. She understood why her dad never had Jackie come around more, if she had seen what was happening to her, she would've reported it... right?

Jinx watched as a glowing white appeared around Jackie, a heat burning into her knee. Jinx hissed through the pain, but after a few minutes, there was nothing there but a faded white scar. She then moved to her arm, Jinx sliding the hidden petals into her other hand as Jackie worked. It was quicker than her knee, the bones popping back into where they were supposed to be.

"Everything else looks good." Jackie smiled weakly. "You must be terrified, you poor thing."

Jinx watched as Thaddeus grabbed Jackie's hand, cupping it to him. His aura turned white while he spoke, Jinx realizing what he was doing. He absorbed some of her power to use later. They were going to put her through extreme torture, then heal her again.

She turned her face away, not letting them see the tears that slid down her cheeks. Jinx had to be strong, she needed to get back to Ren, and together, they could do something about the abuse the Heroes had put her through.

"If you need anything else, let me know." Jackie smiled before disappearing into the fire.

Packard's faked smile dropped from his face, snarling at Jinx. "Chain her up."

Jinx struggled as both Thaddeus and Micha launched at her, holding down each of her extremities to chain her to the bed. Once done, they stepped away, Packard leaning against the wall next to her.

"This is how things are going to work," Packard said, looking at his nails, "You will give us information, and we won't torture you. If you refuse, we will torture you to the brink of death, then Thaddeus will heal you." Jinx shuttered, clenching her teeth together. She would not talk. "Micha, would you like to start?" Packard asked with a smile as if offering him dessert.

Micha nodded, looking nervously between Packard and Jinx. "What does Ren have planned?"

Jinx stayed quiet.

"Answer him Jinx, you don't have to get hurt." Packard said, a joy in his tone. "You know what I am capable of." She looked away from them, clutching the petals in her hands. "Fine, have it your way." Packard hissed.

He took a key, unlocking the ends of the cuffs from the bedframe, looping them together. He did the same to her feet, taking her by the hair and throwing her off the bed. Jinx stumbled, holding onto the base of the hair he held, trying to free herself. She didn't deserve this, she didn't do anything wrong.

He threw her to the ground, taking the end of her chains and tying a rope through it. He went to a tree, where the rope had been strung over a set of pullies and tied to a hook.

"Micha, you're the strongest, pull Jinx up to about halfway." He said casually. Micha stared at him with an open mouth gaping like a fish out of water. "Don't make me repeat myself." Packard growled.

Micha walked hesitantly to the tree and began pulling at the rope. Jinx quickly placed the petals into her jean's pocket, she couldn't lose them.

The rope forced Jinx up, her hands grabbing onto the chains, so the shackles did not break her wrists. Her feet kicked in the air, their chain clanking on the hard dirt beneath her. She shuttered, her tears coming down her face in streams.

"Rip her shirt off, it will be harder to heal if there's cloth in the wounds." Packard ordered.

Thaddeus lifted a knife up to her, cutting away a knit sweater Ren had bought her. A sweater he had given to her because she told him how she preferred them over dresses. He ripped it off her, exposing her stomach and back, the sleeves still on her arms, strands of gray yarn drifting over her.

"Ugh, what happened to her back?" Micha asked scrunching his nose up in disgust.

"A Villain got to her," Packard lied, "And now she's on their side."

"I don't understand that, Jinx, how could you be so idiotic as to trust them?" Micha said, anger in his voice.

She closed her eyes, crying, swinging in the air with her body exposed. Jinx refused to look as she heard the whip snap, the usual way her father always started the beatings. She shielded her face down, her body tensing as she knew what was coming.

The whip cracked out over her skin, blood pouring over the old wounds as a new one was created. She screamed, head flying back from the pain.

Another hit.

Then another.

Then another.

Packard had whipped her until her back was no better looking than ground meat. Only the assault didn't stop, he got tired. He passed the whip to Thaddeus, Jinx barely able to hear anything past the pain that radiated over her body.

Then it started again.

Her head bobbed, eyes fluttering as each slice brought her back to consciousness. There was blood and skin piled beneath her, her arms losing their grip on the chains that held her in the air. Jinx couldn't cry, she only focused on holding her hands around those metal links above her.

She closed her eyes, thinking back to Ren making her breakfast in the morning. How it felt for him to wrap his arm around her shoulders. She saw his smile and through the trees, she saw the soft green glow of his power, leading her to him. She knew the way back if she was able to survive. Her eyes flashed open, a new motivation to withstand the pain. She needed to get back to Ren.

Each crack of the whip sent more pain into her, each moment of searing pain building a fire of anger within the core of her soul. It went on for hours until there was not one part of her back that was left untouched. Her flesh was exposed and she was left there, hanging by the shackles of her wrists.

Every time she moved, the pain would drift over her body. Blood still dripped from her back, the blood loss making her head bob into unconsciousness.

She had to stay awake.

If she didn't—

She would lose hold of—

Jinx's eyes closed, her body going limp and her hands falling from the chains. The shackles cut into her wrists, a new exit for the blood to escape from.

Jinx Dorian hung from that tree as a thunderstorm ripped through the forest. Each swing from the wind sending more and more pain over her body. Eventually, her shoulders popped out of the joint, her scapula easily tearing through the thin muscle she had left on her back.

There was no Heroism in this act against her. No evil these men overcame. The sorting had been wrong, until that night, Jinx had been neutral, neither good nor bad. But as she swung there, body soaked in the rain that froze her blood and turned her fingers blue, she knew who her enemies were.

Jinx was not born to be a Villain. She was created to be one.

Thaddeus had been unable to heal Jinx fully, mainly focusing on the dislocated shoulders and protruding scapulars. They placed a dirty cloth over her bag, wrapping gauze around her waist and chest to hold it there.

The torture didn't stop.

While not whipping her, Micha had been sent to fill a trough of water. Her arms were still sore when her father had force her to kneel over it.

The most awful thing about the entire situation is there was always one question. There was not a series of questions, or any repeated. One question, one chance to answer.

"How did Ren brainwash you?" Thaddeus asked. He honestly believed she was under the influence of some spell. But Jinx kept quiet, biting her lip.

"Put her under."

Micha forced her head under the water, her chest slamming hard against the wooden trough, all the air she had held in vanished. Her lungs burned as she tried to hold off breathing, but instinct took over and she inhaled. Water was the only thing she breathed in, her lungs screaming in agony. She tried to push against the side of the trough, but there was no use, Micha had a strong hold on her. Her body began to twitch, her movements going limp when her head was pulled backwards, and air filled her.

She rolled to her side, coughing up the water she had inhaled. Her breathing sounded raspy, wet hair hanging in clumped strings down her cheeks and bunched in her neck. The dirt on the ground stuck to the water on her face, Jinx breathing in deeply as tears dripped from her eyes.

Jinx only got a few minutes before Micha and Thaddeus picked her up from the ground. She fought against them, tearing open some of the healing parts of her back, the blood seeping through the sheet.

"I am innocent!" She screamed. "I didn't do anything wrong but be born into this family."

Micha and Thaddeus hesitated, looking between Jinx then one another.

"Put her in the water." Packard ordered.

"You're worse than the Villains!" Jinx screamed. "They would never do this to me. You're evil!"

She gasped, her head forced into the water. She held her breath as long as she could. Past the point where her lungs begged her to resurface, pushing through the tensed muscles and cramping her body began to experience. She let it out, gasping once again for air that was not there.

Jinx could handle the beatings, a lack of food, dehydration, but this, being deprived of oxygen, was the worst thing she had ever gone through. The water burned as it entered her lungs, she could feel every inch of her body suffering each second she was under. Her sight became blurry and she was pulled from the water.

She stopped fighting them after several relays of them forcing her under the water. Jinx was nothing to them. She had been sorted as a Background Character, a meaningless person who lived and worked in Central City. She was only changed due to Thaddeus, who now planned to kill her when his quest was originally to save her. Ironic how things worked out.

Micha and Thaddeus had to drag Jinx back into the cabin, not throwing her onto the stained bed like before, but a tiny room off to the side from the fireplace. She fell against the wall as they forced her inside, sliding down it slowly, her body too weak to stand. She heard a clicking of a lock, a small keyhole allowed for a fraction of light into the space.

Crossing her arms over herself, she rested her head against the wall. With her back burning and her entire body aching, Jinx began to formulate a plan. All she had to do was fall asleep and everything would fall into place.

Chapter Ten
Background Character Hospitality

Jinx counted the times the sun had peaked through the key hole. Seven. Seven days, she had been in that room. The door was opened twice in those seven days, a can of food opened halfway for her.

She had never been so hungry in her life, the food tasting better than any meal Ren had ever made her. Jinx didn't know what the food she had been eating was, though she stacked the cans neatly in the corner of the closet.

It was a fun challenge she made for herself, to see how long she could produce magic until she couldn't manage even a small spark to her finger. The flowers, however, stayed invisible. She could feel them there in her pants, not drying out or flaking. It was as if they knew they would be needed and stayed pristine for her.

Micha would leave some days, not coming back until late. Peering through the keyhole she saw the injuries he had suffered, Jinx smiling before sitting back, knowing that Ren would not stop until he had her again. That was how she was able to sleep, the knowledge of Ren tearing apart Central City. What she wouldn't give to just see his face.

Footsteps approached her, Jinx laying her head against the wall and closing her eyes. Nine days since she arrived, Ren's favorite number.

The door opened, Thaddeus standing there with a can of food.

"Thaddeus?" Jinx said in a small voice, "Is that you?"

"Jinx?" He asked, hopeful.

"Where am I?" She asked as she forced tears down her face. "I-I don't remember-."

"Hey, hey, it's okay." Thaddeus soothed.

Jinx sniffed. "What happened to my back, it hurts so bad."

Thaddeus shook his head. "You got kidnapped, Jinny. Villains got to you before I could." A pathetic attempt at a lie.

She pouted her lip, forcing her chin to wobble. "Why can't I remember?"

"What's going on?" Packard asked.

"Daddy?" Jinx cried, "I'm sorry I didn't mean to get kidnapped; I can't remember what happened."

It wasn't hard for Jinx to sob; her emotions easily formed a knot in her throat. All she had to do was think hard enough and it would start. The real challenge was not to look at her father with the hate she had for him.

"You don't remember anything?" He asked, raising an eyebrow.

Jinx shook her head, wiping the tears from her eyes. "I was at the bank and then there was a break in. There was a fight-." She shook her head, squeezing her eyes shut. "Daddy, I'm scared."

Packard sighed, rubbing his head. "Untie her, she was clearly entranced."

Jinx forced the smile that begged to be let out down. For being Heroes, they were all stupid.

Thaddeus cut the ropes on Jinx's wrists, a purple bruise encircled around them. She rubbed her wrists as Thaddeus cut the ropes from her ankles. When he was done, she wrapped her arms around his neck, encasing him in a hug. He gently held her back, causing a stinging sensation.

He helped Jinx stand, his body supporting hers. While most of the act was faked, her walking wasn't. Her muscles were sore, cramping from finally being able to extend to their full length. Thaddeus set her on a bench, Jinx looking down to the floor.

"What is she doing out?" Micha asked, coming through the door.

The sun was setting outside, the end of day Nine.

Micha had a large gash bleeding down the side of his head. He held his side which was wrapped in a large white gauze. His suit was ripped and one eye blackened, beginning to swell.

Jinx put her hands to her mouth, eyes watering. "What happened to you?"

He jerked his head back looking to Packard and Thaddeus for answers.

"She was entranced, few days away from Valder and she's good as new." Thaddeus smiled lovingly to her.

"Who's Valder?" Jinx asked, looking between the four men. "I can only remember a kid in my class, Ken, I think."

"Ren Valder, my nemesis." Micha snarled.

Jinx gave the best puppy dog eyes to Micha, practicing the damsel look she had been taught to perfection by her mother. "Did you fight him for me? I-I'm only a Background Character, I'm not worth all this."

Jinx watched as Micha too, fell for her act, his face softening.

"Don't worry, Ms. Dorian, we will protect you." Micha said proudly.

"I'm so lucky to have so many Heroes around me." Jinx smiled weakly. "But my back hurts so badly."

"Micha, get the first aid kit, let's see if our aspiring doctor can walk us through healing." Packard smiled.

Jinx gave her best doe eyed look to her father as Micha ran and retrieved a bag full of medical equipment. She told them how to undress the wounds, the dirty sheet ripped from her back rougher than she would've liked.

"Looking at it, is there any blackened parts or puffy red areas with white stuff leaking out?" She needed to be sure her back wasn't infected.

"Mm, there is a brown piece here." Micha said.

She sighed shakily. "Take the scissors in the bag and cut it off. It'll be bad if it stays on."

There was no hesitation as Thaddeus cut off a chunk of her skin, placing it on the discarded sheet on the table. She almost cried when she saw the brown part he was referring to was only dirt covered skin.

"Now, I need you to wash the area down with clean water." Her voice shook.

They poured the water over her from a pail. She prayed it wasn't the one that had been by the bed when she first arrived. Jinx instructed them how to bandage her correctly, and Thaddeus offered her an extra shirt he had in his bag to cover herself with. She had carefully cut the side fabric of what remained of her bra. Slowly, she pulled the remaining piece through the newly bandaged skin, tossing it to the ground and leaning over the table. The pain radiated over her body, sending spirals of it through her extremities.

Micha and her father had stepped out, doing god knows what. She was left with Thaddeus. How lucky that was.

"Thad," Jinx said weakly. He walked to her, helping her sit down. "I need tea."

"Tea?" He asked.

She nodded. "There are herbs within some cinnamon tea that helps heal. I can make it, I learned how to, I just need the ingredients."

Thaddeus bit his lip, nodding. "I'll ask Micha when he goes back to the city."

Jinx sighing, letting loose a look of pain. She breathed in harshly, placing her hand to her back. "It hurts." She whimpered.

Thaddeus stood, walking to the door. "Cinnamon tea?"

Jinx nodded, tears falling down her cheeks.

He walked out the door, closing it behind him.

Jinx crossed her arms over her stomach, her shoulder shaking as she silently cried. She just wanted to get back to Ren, then everything would be okay. She had a plan for the tea, had a plan to leave, but she had to be patient. What she was finding was patience wasn't her strong suit.

Her stomach churned and she rushed to the door. Micha and Packard were walking back to the cabin, arms filled with logs. She bent her body over, emptying the minimal contents of her stomach onto the ground in the most pitiful puddle.

"Are you feeling okay?" Micha asked, stopping before entering the door.

Jinx nodded weakly. "I'll be okay once Thad gets back with the healing tea."

He furrowed his brows but nodded, walking into the cabin. She spit at the ground, holding her stomach as she walked back into her prison hold. She needed Thaddeus to come back soon.

"When did you learn to make tea?" Packard asked, watching Jinx as she stirred the ingredients into a kettle.

"When I became a Background Character. It was difficult to learn but became a hobby." She smiled weakly. "I think it's best if Micha drinks some too, he did get hurt fighting the man who kidnapped me. It's the least I can do."

Micha nodded, smirking as he leaned forward in his seat.

"Can someone get me some mugs?" She asked.

Packard got up from his position on the bench, grabbing four mugs from a bag.

Jinx furrowed her brows. "Four?"

"Well I have to try this tea my daughter learned to make with healing qualities, don't I?" He smiled.

Jinx chuckled, setting the metal mugs on the floor in front of her. She had torn a hole in her pants, shoving the petals to the tips of her pocket for easy access.

She went for the kettle, touching the rim, pulling back as if it was hot. She rubbed her hand against her pant leg collecting the petals like sorting through cards. Her heart skipped a beat as she felt through the petals. Five? No, she had six before, she was sure of it. Her mind scanned through her knowledge of *venenum flos*, what happens with only one petal?

She waved her hand over the mugs, feeling as two petals dropped into each one, except for the third which only had one petal. Grabbing a cloth, she removed the tea from the fire, pouring the cinnamon scented water into all four cups. Jinx rose from the floor, handing a cup to each man. When getting to Packard, he raised his hand at the mug.

"I thought you wanted one?" She asked softly, looking into the cup.

"I want that one." He said, pointing to the other one she didn't offer to him.

She furrowed her brows, nodding, and handed him the mug she had planned to keep for herself. Jinx slowly sat herself on the floor, aware that Packard watched her every move.

Lifting the cup to her lips, she drank a large gulp. The three boys then tasted their own, humming in surprise. She hadn't known what the flowers tasted like, but assumed the cinnamon taste in the bread was a good guess, masking the taste with a cinnamon tea.

"This is decent, Jinny, good job." Packard smiled.

Jinx tipped her cup to her lips again, smiling into it. She had known her dad wouldn't have trusted her so easily, holding back the cup with the petals for herself.

As she finished her drink, she laid in front of the fire, waiting for the poison to take its effect. Micha was the first to go, slumping onto the table, hand still on his cup.

"Keep watch, I'm going to bed." Packard said, laying down on the stained bed in the corner.

Both were handed cups with double petals, but Thaddeus stayed awake, if barely. He watched the fire, his eyelids bobbing up and down, trying to stay awake.

"Thad, are you still awake?" Jinx asked softly.

"Yeah." He smiled lazily.

She rolled over, patting the floor beside her. "Can you tell me how your powers work?"

He slunk over to her, laying with his back down. "It's nothing fancy," He slurred, "All I do is think of their power moving into my hand and presto, new ability."

She laid her head and his shoulder, feeling him relax. "Does it ever go away? The power you absorb I mean."

He shrugged. "Depends on the power. Dad's stayed, but I'm in close contact with him. The others never do last long."

She nodded. The information was good to know and report back to Ren when she escapes. "Hey, Thad, can you fly with me? I've always wanted to, but never got to with dad."

Thaddeus sighed. "I don't know, Jinny, if dad finds out we're screwed."

Jinx lifted off his chest. "I promise not to tell, it'll be like summer break before my sorting." She smiled as brightly as she could. "Please, Thad, I need something to liven me up."

He rolled his eyes smiling. "I could never turn down that smile of yours."

Micha and Packard didn't so much as stir as a lethargic Thaddeus and scheming Jinx walked out the door. Thaddeus lifted Jinx into his grasp, her back pressed against his arm, making her want to scream in pain. She fought against it, smiling at him.

"Where to?" He asked with a sleepy smile.

Jinx placed a finger to her lip as if thinking. "There's an ice cream shop in Central City open all night, can we go there?" She knew there was not such a place, but Thaddeus wouldn't.

"Jinx-."

"The owners know me, they won't get involved with anything." Jinx pleaded.

Thaddeus sighed, jogging and jumping into the air, flying them in the direction of Central City. With one petal, a person was so sleep hazy, their own objections can be surpassed with a simple argument and pretty smile. With her obsession over the flower, Jinx was determined to write a book about it once her world calmed down again.

It only took ten minutes to get from the cabin to Central City, though she wouldn't have known it from the destruction. Entire skyscrapers had tumbled to nothing but rubble, streets she normally walked to work on encased in the debris. There was a crater in the middle of the bank, nothing but the white columns remaining of the structure. Everything was gone or surrounded by destruction.

Jinx pursed her lips, concealing a smile. Ren did this for her.

A camera crew was stationed below them, Jinx getting her idea like a light shining in a bulb.

"The ice cream shop is still standing!" She gleamed, pointing not to an ice cream shop, but a consignment store she had bought her dress she wore to the re-sorting from. The television crew next to it.

Thaddeus didn't object as they landed and of course, as she planned, the crew began recording him, walking up to ask him questions. Jinx, only a bystander in the background. A perfect Background Character.

"Have you had any news on your nemesis, Mr. Dorian?" One reporter asked, putting a microphone towards Thaddeus.

"Uh, no, not yet." He said weakly, eyes blinking from the camera light pinned on him.

"And what of Ren Valder, will you help defeat him with Michanis?" They asked.

Michanis? Jinx thought, *What a lame Hero name.*

"Ren Valder is public enemy number one, we will stop him in the name of justice." Thaddeus said as rehearsed by their parents.

The city is safe in the Dorian family name. Jinx thought in her head.

"The city is safe in the Dorian family name." Thaddeus smiled, his chest puffing.

Jinx smiled, keeping down the laugh she wanted to throw out. But where was Ren? He should have seen her by now.

In the distance, an explosion rang out.

She looked up as a building a few blocks away crumbled. The police station. Her eyes lit up, knowing that Ren had come for her. She turned to Thaddeus, instantly molding into her sweet innocent persona. "We have to help those people!"

Thaddeus clenched his jaw, looking between her and the camera that was aimed at him, reporters staring at him expectantly. "Stay safe!" He said, shooting into the air and flying towards the building.

Jinx took off running.

The reporters called after her, but she didn't care about them. Ren was here and he would save her.

There was a glowing smile over her face as she looked for him, but both him and Thaddeus were no where to be found. Jinx circled the block several times, her lungs stinging having not yet recovered from the water torture.

That's when she heard banging.

She ran towards it, walking into the sorting auditorium.

It was dark, no lights turned on as she shimmied her way through the seats. An eerie blue spotlight hung down onto the circular crest on the ground, Jinx walking towards it. There were no other noises that could relate to the banging she heard before.

She hopped onto the stage, her body screaming in protest as the wounds on her back once again split open. Blood leaked through the bandage and into Thaddeus' large shirt. Her hair was unruly and matted, not having been kept up or brushed. Her jeans were covered with dried blood, face and exposed body covered in remnants of mud. For how she looked, Thaddeus was a fool for ever bringing her out to Central City.

"You're a liar, aren't you?" She asked the glowing light. "Just a machine with no other function than to split society." She walked around the blue light, looking at the art on the floor beneath it. "You made my father a Hero, but he was a monster. Same with Thaddeus and Micha, both should've been Henchmen for how they followed his every order." She chuckled, skipping around the outline. "You told me I was no one the first time, then you told me I was both good and bad. So, I want to know," Jinx stopped, stepping into the glowing blue light. "What am I now?"

The voice was loud, echoing down the streets. "Jinx Dorian. Age: twenty-four. Previous sort: Background Character. Previous sort: Morally Gray. Sorting."

Jinx bounced, her hands behind her back as she waited. To the left entrance, she saw her brother rush in, covered in gray plaster and a stream of blood down his face. On the right was Ren.

He looked equally as awful, normally slick hair matted to the side of his head, a wound allowing blood to cover his entire ear. There was a thick cut on his right eye, going down his forehead and ending at his cheek. His eyes locked to her, a crazed look to them.

Above her, the light turned.

She smiled, not needing to hear the voice as it spoke her sort. She laughed, doubling over in the spotlight, cackling like a mad woman.

"Villain."

Her ear pointed up, listening for the person who would become her enemy. Equal and destined to die by her hand.

"Hero match: Thaddeus Dorian."

Her smile didn't leave as her eyes went to her brother. The look on his face was priceless. Everything over the look was filled with regret and despair, he was, after all, the reason for her change, in more ways than just that stupid quest.

"Happy, brother?" She spit.

"You were supposed to be a Hero." He stammered.

"Who wants to be a Hero when you willingly beat your own flesh and blood?" Jinx jumped from the stage, clicking her tongue. "Hope you realize what's coming for you, Thaddeus. You've seen nothing of what I am capable of."

Jinx turned from him quickly, running to Ren who opened his arms to her. She jumped, latching onto his neck. When she kissed him, she had been in the sorting auditorium, but pulling away, they were in the dark, damp cave of his family home.

Jinx laughed, her legs wrapping around him, hands splayed through his hair. "Fuck, it's really you."

He laughed, pressing a hard kiss to her lips. "I looked for you everywhere."

"You tore Central City apart for me." She giggled.

His hands lifted her shirt, stopping at the poorly wrapped bandages there. "Jinx."

She already knew it wasn't worth the fight, turning and lifting the shirt so it only covered her breasts. "They did a poor job wrapping it, I may need your mom's help."

She noticed the blood that had soaked the shirt, looking back to Ren. His eyes had gone black, his power radiating off of him, causing a bright glow. She placed the shirt back over her, spinning to him.

"Hey, hey," She said, cupping his cheek. "Ren look at me."

His eyes darted to her, still full of hatred. "I'm alive. Micha and my father are comatose. We have time."

"How much time?" He fumed.

"However much time two *venenum flos* petals gives us."

Some green returned to his eyes as they traced over her face. "How did you manage that?"

Jinx grinned, wiggling side to side. "I learned how to make things disappear."

Ren laughed, throwing his head back. He stared at her, grabbing her by the nape. "Jinx Dorian, I am madly in love with you."

Jinx smiled, her face close to his, her lips brushing softly over them. "Ren Valder, you're not going to believe this," She smiled, biting her lip. "You're my weakness."

Chapter Eleven
Much Needed Respite

Jinx had hissed a breath through her teeth as a Henchman with healing experience had slowly ripped off the bandage to her back. Knox, Ren's father, had a firm hold on his son's shoulder, but Jinx knew that if he saw the slightest increase in pain from her, the Henchman would be dead.

"This isn't good." The Henchman said, Jinx turning to see him shaking his head.

"Infection?" She asked. It was a possibility due to the disgusting blanket that had originally covered the wound.

"No, there's no skin left. There are bits around the edges, but I can't heal something that has to regrow muscle and skin." He said nervously. "What happened to you?"

"Heroes." Jinx growled. "The real fucking monsters."

The Henchman tightened his lips, looking to Knox. "Sir, with your help it may not be as traumatic."

Jinx looked to Knox whose jaw tensed.

"What would you need?" He asked, though his voice didn't give Jinx an impression of anger, it was more sorrow.

The Henchman looked to Jinx with remorse. "In order for me to grow new skin for her, I need to speed up her healing process. It will be painful."

Knox nodded, moving from his son to Jinx. "I don't know if this will work, your power may deflect it."

Jinx nodded, grinding her teeth. "Let me try something."

She lifted her arm, focusing on the shield around her body. The transparent orange light flickered over her, shimmering as Thaddeus' clear energy had. Jinx closed her eyes, willing the light to expand over Knox and the Henchman, both looking unnerved as they felt it pass over them.

"You should be okay now, I think I surrounded you in my barrier."

Knox raised his eyebrows, nodding once. He placed both his hands on the sides of her head, the black tips of his fingers extending down his hands and over his arms. "You won't feel a thing."

Jinx's mind was cleared of everything. She was no longer in the kitchen with Ren, Knox, and the Henchman, but the beach house her family owned. She hadn't been to it in years, barely even remembered it was a thing.

Her eyes sparkled as she walked towards the water, smiling as she dipped her toes in. The chill of the water climbed up her leg, leaving goosebumps in its wake. She moved past the water, going to the dock where her small sailboat still stood, brand new and never abandoned. Her hand danced along the side of the wood, pink paint presenting the name of it, *The Escape.*

It had been part of her plan when she was younger, to leave Honorville and travel up north to see what other life she could have. A dream that had never come true.

She walked into the cabin, smiling at the drawings she had left on the table. Her on the sailboat, swimming in the water, her head being dunked into a trough. Fear encompassed her, the smile fading from her face. Where was her father? If she was here, he had to be close, right? The scars on her back burned as if the wounds were brand new. Her breathing increased, spinning in the lake house. She wasn't safe, she wouldn't be safe as long as she was in Honorville.

"Jinx." Ren's voice came from the door. She turned, seeing him, no longer in the cabin, but somewhere unknown.

A river trickled over rocks behind her, being fed by small drainage from the giant mountains around them. Ren stood in front of a stone building built inside of the mountain. It was curved and instead of clear windows, stained glass took their place.

"What is this place?" She asked, rushing to cling to his arm.

"The location of my fondest memories." He smiled.

"How did we get here?"

"It's not important."

She furrowed her brows but nodded. She trusted him.

He led her towards the main entrance, his arm lifting over her shoulders, hand entangled in hers as they walked. She could smell his soothing scent of lemon balm and lavender, something her mother would claim is a feminine smell, but fits him nonetheless.

Ren held the door open for her, and she marveled at the beauty inside. The windows decorated the room in multiple colors, the furniture making her feel like she could easily fall asleep on it. A fireplace was carved into a rock wall, the skin of a bear positioned in front of it, books stacked in piles around the creature. Artwork lined the walls, and a portrait of Ren rested over the hearth, displaying the cocky grin she adored.

He grabbed her hand, smiling as he walked down a corridor. Instead of the electric lights she was used to, gas lamps lit the otherwise dark hall. They flickered with a blue light, reminding her of the flowers outside the window of her library. He turned into a room, a beautiful kitchen that surpassed the one at Valder Manor. The countertops were ivory, appliances stainless steel. Pots and pans hung from a rack above the island, a black kettle resting over the stove. The room smelled like fresh bread and coffee, making her mouth water. How long had it been since she had a coffee?

She could see him in the kitchen making her meals, her sitting on the counter while he did so, his hand resting on her leg.

"There's more to see." He said, leading her away from the kitchen, down the opposite hall. He passed multiple doors, each carved with different displays.

Turning, he opened at door at the end of the hall, colorful light dancing over the insides. It was a ballroom, not large like the one they had first danced in, but big enough for her. A piano sat on a small stage, papers filled with music notes waiting to be played. The floor was a checkered black and white, the white now colored in green, red, and yellow.

"Do you play piano?" She asked with a smile.

"Of my many talents, musical instruments are not one." He laughed. She embraced the sound of his laugh as it echoed in the room. God how she loved his laugh.

He moved to another room, one they had passed going to the ballroom. There were no windows in this one, light brought to her in glowing orange flames of gas lanterns.

A four poster bed sat in the center, over hardwood floors that looked old and worn. Silken drapes hung from the canopy placed above the bed, silver sheets exposed within. Two dark wooden night tables rested beside the bed, glowing *venenum flos* displayed in an opaque blue vase on one of them. While not as expansive as the library, several bookshelves lined the far wall, new books she had not yet been able to discover.

"Is this-."

"Our bedroom." He smiled softly.

"Our?" She asked.

He chuckled. "I do plan on spending the rest of our lives together, Dorian."

She smiled, it reaching her eyes. "Our entire lives? You might get sick of me at some point."

He shook his head. "I have been in love with you since school, my dear. I have seen many changes from you, and I have never once faltered in that feeling."

"I wish you would've stolen me away sooner." She giggled, nuzzling into his side.

"You have no idea how much I wanted to."

She closed her eyes, embracing the feeling of his arms around her. "I'm so happy you're mine."

He kissed the top of her forehead, breathing deeply as he did.

"Ren, why do I feel funny, like this is all fake?" She asked.

Opening her eyes, the room seemed to shift. Something was off about it, but she couldn't figure out what. She looked to the side, and Ren was gone. She was back at the beach house, alone.

Jinx didn't know what was happening, her body felt as if she was on fire. She fell to the floor, her nails digging into the polished wood. She hurt all over, like she was experiencing the pain of the whipping, only in reverse.

Then she went numb.

She felt nothing, her face relaxing. She fell to the side, curling herself into a ball. She wasn't in the beach house anymore, but the yellow bedroom of her childhood home. Jinx was wrapped in purple blankets, a yellow comforter with daisies embroidered into it placed over her.

Past the pink door, she heard her father screaming. He had lost to Demented Doom again. She prayed he was drunk, then he would only use his belt. She quickly shoved a small blanket into her shirt and pants, waiting for the door to burst open.

When it did, her father was dripping sweat, his eyes crazed. He slipped the belt off his pants, gripping the leather looped side instead of the buckle. She squeezed her eyes shut, begging internally for someone to save her, but she knew no one ever would.

The beating didn't hurt like it normally did, the motion only feeling like a pulsing. Relief flooded her, and she relaxed into her pillow until he finished. He wiped the sweat from his mouth, stomping out the door.

Her mother came in soon after, picking out clothes for her to wear to school that same day. A teal dress with white stockings. She dressed quickly, applied the makeup that was simple, yet beautiful. Her mother had put her hair into curls down her back, no one would notice the deformation that way. Then Jinx was sent to school.

She was thirteen. Skinny and tall for her age, but still elegant either way. She found her class, looking over the other students nervously.

"Class, this is Jinx Dorian, please welcome her as our new student." The teacher had announced. She had been the new student because of her family name. For fear that she would be kidnapped as a child for who she was connected to. "Jinx, you can sit in any empty seat."

She walked to a chair in the third row, third seat back. Jinx kept her back straight, looking ahead and not speaking a word all morning. When lunch had come around, she had followed the other kids to the cafeteria, only to be stopped by one pushing her into the lockers.

He was brutish with red hair and a nasty snarl across his face. "Another Hero destined Dorian, how wonderful."

"Please excuse me, I have to go to lunch." She said weakly.

"Polite too, what a Love Interest thing to say." Two boys on either side of him laughed, each looking to her cruelly.

"I-I don't know what I did wrong, but I apologize." She squeaked.

"That's enough." A dark voice said from behind them.

The bullies paled, scurrying away quickly.

Jinx looked to the boy who saved her, deathly pale skin with black hair slicked back from his face. His eyes changed from a dark green to emerald as he looked upon her, his lips in a tight line.

"How can you be a child from the Dorian family if you don't defend yourself?" He spit.

Jinx looked down. "They want me to be a Love Interest."

"And what do you want to be?"

Jinx looked at the boy surprised. She had never been asked what she wanted, only told what she should be. She smiled softly thinking of what life she would want for herself. One that was easy, that would let her get out of Honorville.

"I want to be a Background Character."

His brows raised, a smirk dancing over his lips. "Interesting choice Dorian, I'll see you around." He walked towards the cafeteria, Jinx reaching out, grabbing his sleeve.

"What's your name?" She asked.

He smiled down at her hand over his shirt, looking back to her. "I'm Ren Valder."

"Thank you, Ren." She said, removing her hand.

He shook his head. "Best not to thank a Villain, you never know what their motives are."

Jinx furrowed her brows, watching as Ren walked away. A kid who wanted to be a Villain but saved her from bullies. What a strange meeting.

Jinx's eyes were filled with tears as she saw Knox remove his hands from her head, looking to her horrified. "I am so sorry."

The Henchman and Ren looked to him in shock, Jinx forcing her eyes to the ground. "It wasn't your fault, he was a monster."

Knox shook his head. "I had a part to play in how you were treated, Jinx. I didn't know, otherwise, I would've taken you away from all of that."

She nodded, unable to do much more.

Jinx hadn't realized Knox would be able to see everything going on inside her head. She felt awful for letting him see what her dad did to her after Knox had only done what he was supposed to. But even so, he would've taken her away. Kidnapped her to a house of safety in Vileterra where she would have been treated with kindness.

"Dad, what are you apologizing for?" Ren asked nervously.

Knox sighed, looking to Ren. "With Jinx's dad being my nemesis, there were days when I would beat him. When there were those days, her dad would come home and take it out on her."

The Henchman walked past Knox, nodding to him, looking to Jinx with pity.

"Why didn't you tell me?" Ren asked, appalled.

Jinx bit her lip. "I didn't want you to look at your dad differently because of how my dad dealt with his losses."

Ren shook his head, walking to her and brought her head to his chest. Jinx was startled, not expecting this reaction after withholding information from him.

"You are too good for this world, Jinx Dorian." He whispered.

She sighed, her hands knotting into his shirt, her head relaxing against his chest. "I saw you, in my head."

Knox chuckled. "The first time you had felt safe with someone."

Ren smiled. "At the bank?"

She shook her head, pulling back. "First day of school, you saved me from bullies." She smiled. "You asked me what I wanted to be sorted into and I said Background Character."

His fingers moved through her hair, still tangled from her torture. "That was the first time you felt safe with someone?"

She nodded. "Eleven years ago you found me, and while I didn't know it, you had been protecting me since then."

"Everyday you stepped foot into Central City, I was there, watching. I had threatened the entire class to not lay a finger on you."

"You threatened the entire class?" She giggled. A smile forming on his lips.

"Of course I did, I had influence even at thirteen."

"No wonder I never could make any friends." She laughed tugging on his shirt. Her smile faded, thinking back to how she had remembered that memory to begin with. "My back, is it…"

"Good as new. Would you like to see?"

She nodded, sliding off the table and following Knox and Ren to a floor to ceiling length mirror in a room she had never seen before. It spanned the entire wall, reminding her of the dance classes she took as a child. She turned, Ren lifting her shirt to expose her back. She placed a hand to her mouth, gasping as she looked.

Jinx had no scars.

Even the old ones had disappeared from her skin, it looked pristine, brand new. There was no evidence of her childhood traumas or torture she had recently endured, only clear untouched skin.

However clear her back looked, inside Jinx knew those scars remained. They had been engrained into her psyche, mutating her mind to remember the hatred those scars caused. The reason she had wanted to become a Background Character as a child.

"They're still there." She whispered, seeing Knox nod in the mirror.

"The physical can be fixed, but not the mind."

She nodded, straightening herself and lifting her head. "I look awful, can I clean up?"

"Of course." Ren smiled sadly, "I'll get everything prepared."

Knox had parted from them as Ren led Jinx to her room, her hand holding his tightly.

He did not let her do anything.

Ren had carried her up the spiral staircase, sat her down on the vanity and picked up her brush. She lifted her hand, uncovering the mirror so she could watch him. He was tender, starting at the ends, working is way up slowly. There was not a moment where he showed resentment in the task, often kissing her temple to put her at ease.

Hair collected on the brush, unable to escape after her father had ripped the locks from her head, leaving them to matte into knots. Ren was patient, not pulling or harming her in anyway as he worked. Once done, He wrapped his arms around her neck, sighing deeply into her head.

She knew how painful this was for him, the guilt that consumed him for letting her get treated like this. She took in a shaking breath, leaning into his embrace, wrapping her hands around his arms.

"I love you." She whispered.

"I love you."

He unwrapped his arms from around her, pulling her up and leading her into her bathroom. Ren let go of her hands, sitting on the edge of the claw foot tub, and turned the faucet on.

The water sent Jinx into a panic.

Her heart pounded and body shook. She backed into the wall, sliding down it as she stared at the water. Flashes of her head being dumped into the trough triggered her to hyperventilate. Her throat burned as if the water was once again making its way into her lungs.

She couldn't breathe. Couldn't escape. She could take the whipping, take the beatings, but she couldn't be in the water again. They would kill her. They wouldn't let her escape now she was a Villain. Her brother's Villain.

"Jinx, hey, look at me." Ren said, fear clear in his voice.

"Don't force me in again-." She pleaded, tears streaming down her face. "I don't want to drown."

She could not tell it was him, staring only at the running water that splashed into the collective beneath it.

His jaw dropped, moving quickly to turn off the water. Her body shook as he returned, moving into her eyeline to block her view of the tub.

"You're okay." He said gently. "I'm here, you're okay now."

Her breathing slowed, looking to him. She felt the shaking of her chin and chattering of her teeth as the fear consumed her. "They-they drowned me." She whispered. "And then they took me out, only to put me back in." She shook her head. "Ren, I almost died. My dad, brother, and Micha almost killed me."

"Micha?" Ren asked with eyes wide.

Jinx nodded. "Micha was helping."

His jaw clenched, his arms wrapping around her tightly. "I'm here, no one will ever hurt you again."

She took a shaking breath. "I want to kill them."

He nodded into her. "Then we will."

"Promise?" She whispered.

"On my life."

Instead of Jinx sitting in the bath, she sat to the side, body still shaking. Ren was behind her, kneeling in the tub, his pants and shirt soaked as he ran the water over her hair. His body blocked the water from splashing into the tub, allowing her to relax slightly.

He helped her undress, respectfully taking a sponge and running it over her body, careful not to let any water drip down her as he did so. She leaned into him as he washed her, Ren never complaining as he continued.

Once cleaned, he dried her with a towel, wrapping her in a fluffy robe. He sat her on the bed while he washed himself off, coming from the bedroom door instead of the bathroom with a clean shirt and pants. She smiled softly, realizing he had teleported to get his clothes.

In his arms, he held a black shirt and a pair of gray shorts. He turned as she changed into them, realizing that this was not her shirt, but his. She lifted the front of it to her nose, inhaling deeply. His scent was embedded into it, calming the nerves that still fluttered within her.

"I'm done." She said, waiting as he turned towards her.

He smiled, gazing at her in his shirt proudly. Walking towards her, he picked up a hair tie off the vanity.

"Sit in the bed." He said.

She followed the order, crossing her legs as she sat, his body moving beside hers. He pulled back her hair, his fingers separating the locks into three sections and began to braid. She closed her eyes, focusing on each movement that he made until tying it off.

"When did you learn to braid?" She asked, leaning back against him.

"We were sixteen, you came to school with this crazy intricate braided crown around your head. While I can't remake that crown, I learned to braid incase one day, you said to me you only ever wanted to wear a braid." He brushed his hand against her face, tracing the outlines of her jaw.

"Everything you've done-."

"Has always been for you."

She twisted around, wrapping her legs around him and hugging him. "Even though your stalking was overboard, I am so happy for it."

He laughed, kissing her head. "I wish you could see yourself the way I do. Your imperfections are perfect to me, your sarcasm like the most beautiful of melodies, and your frown, equivalent to a knife in my chest."

"Stay with me," She begged, "Don't make me sleep alone without you."

He brought his knuckle to her chin, lifting her eyes to look to him. "I promised you whatever you wanted, staying beside you is the least I can do."

Ren kept his promise. He had laid beside Jinx, wrapping her in his arms, their foreheads touching as they were intertwined with one another. In those moments, where Jinx was encompassed in Ren's arms, there were no Villains or Heroes, no world outside of their own.

In Ren's arms, Jinx was safe.

Chapter Twelve
White

When Jinx had woken, Ren was not by her side. In a panic, she scrambled down the stairs, pausing as she hit the floor of the library. Ren sat in a chair, his leg crossed over the other, a book in his hand as he sipped from a black mug. On the side table, as normal, her gray mug sat, steam rising from the coffee inside.

It was the routine.

He had not forgotten, doing what they always had every morning. And in that moment, she realized, he had been taking part in this routine because it was what she needed. It was what she had been used to all those years after her sorting. The same pattern everyday at a specific time. While she had Morally Gray at that point, he made her transition to life in Vileterra easier by giving her this routine. A sign of his love before there ever was an idea of it in her head.

She smiled, walking to him. He lifted his eyes to greet her, her head lowering and planting a long kiss to his lips. He chuckled as she walked to her seat, picking up her book and sipping her perfectly made coffee.

"How do you take your coffee?" She asked, a small detail she wanted to know. She tilted her head back, the sloppy braid falling back over the arm rest.

He smirked, putting his book down. "White."

"White?" She laughed.

"I have possibly one small drop of coffee in my mug, the rest is warmed cream."

Jinx flipped around, not believing a word he said. "Let me see."

He handed her his cup, and just like he said, it was white. She put it to her mouth sipping it and cringing. "This is awful."

"Milk makes your bones big and strong." He smirked.

"And pure cream makes you fat." She retorted.

He lifted his shirt, looking down at his muscles that rolled beneath. "I think I'm okay."

Jinx bit her lip, staring.

"I wanted to wait for you to get up, but there is something I wanted to show you." He smiled. "We will be gone for a few weeks, but we'll be okay."

Jinx frowned, worry covering her. "It's because it isn't safe here anymore, isn't it?"

He grimaced. "Yeah, it is."

She nodded her head, biting her lip. As much as she hated the idea of leaving the manor, the place that had become her home, she wanted them to be safe.

"Are your parents coming?" She asked.

"No, they want to stay and protect our home, but insisted we go." He said.

"When do we leave?"

"As soon as you're dressed." He smiled.

Jinx stood from her chair, ruffling Ren's slicked back hair as she passed him. He shook his head, but the smile on his lips sent butterflies in her stomach.

As she stood in her closet, she noticed most of her clothes were missing. There was a sweater laid out for her, a pair of fleece lined leggings, and fur boots. She furrowed her brows at the outfit, but put it on anyway, figuring Ren was taking her somewhere cold.

She walked to her room, undoing the braid that Ren had placed in her hair the night before. She touched each loop, slowly unfurling it as she remembered how gentle he was putting it in. That's when she heard the talking down stairs.

She went down the steps slowly, listening to the conversation.

"Come on Ren, we used to have so much fun together." A woman's voice pouted.

"I don't want you, Kandace, how much clearer do I have to make that?" Ren growled.

"That Dorian girl doesn't know you like I do. She doesn't know how to make you feel like I do." The woman said slyly.

Jinx walked down the stairs, a snarl on her lips.

The woman was short, her features angular and sharp. Her golden skin complemented her silver eyes, straight white hair stopping at her shoulders. Her outfit was tight, cleavage and stomach exposed. Her short skirt showing her thighs, knee high black boots covering the rest of her.

Jinx didn't make her presence a secret, but due to years of stealth training, this woman, Kandace, never heard her coming.

"I'm going to ask you to step away from him." Jinx snarled.

Kandace jumped, spinning to see Jinx standing behind her, arms crossed and chin held high.

Kandace smirked, looking her over with a judgmental stare. "She is the one you have as your weakness?" She scoffed.

"I am going to say it one more time. Step away."

"Or what," Kandace laughed, "What will your goody-two-shoes ass do to a naturally born-."

Jinx grabbed Kandace by the throat, throwing her to the floor. The wood beneath her head splintered, Jinx kneeling down, pressing her hand tighter on her neck.

"He is mine. Understand?"

The woman nodded, mouth opened as she attempted to gasp for air.

Jinx stood, kicking the woman in the stomach. "Leave."

There was no hesitation from her as she ran into the hall beyond the library.

"Old fling of yours?" Jinx asked with her lips pursed.

Ren walked to her, wrapping his hands around her waist, sliding them across her stomach. His head dropped, lips brushing over her ear. "Something like that."

"If she comes back, I'm going to kill her." Jinx hissed.

"Just make sure I'm there to watch. Nothing is sexier than you besting my old partners." He smirked.

Jinx scoffed, but moved her head to the side, letting him have more access to her skin.

"So distracted you never even realized we teleported." He smirked.

Jinx furrowed her brows, looking around her. Her mouth dropped open, an excited smile appearing on her lips. She forgot about everything that had happened, her mood switching almost immediately.

"It's snowing!" She exclaimed.

Ren raised an eyebrow. "That's what you take from this?"

She left his embrace, tracing her finger through the cold fluff that crunched beneath her. "It's real snow, like actual snow."

He cocked his head to the side. "Doesn't it snow in Honorville?"

"I was never allowed outside when it did, the house was surrounded in a field that melted the snow away." She giggled picking up handfuls. "This is the first time I've ever gotten to touch it!"

She tilted her head up to the sky, letting the snowflakes collect on her eyelashes. The white specks coated her sweater and hair as she looked back to Ren.

His green eyes looked brilliant in the light that reflected off the surface. The white flakes hovering in his hair. There was a peacefulness about his expression, a glance he gave her that made her whole body warm.

Jinx ran to him, jumping into his arms and kissed him. It was not like before, her hands running through his hair, lips parting to allow him in. His hands grabbed onto her back, holding her steady as he walked, Jinx not knowing or caring where he was taking her.

The doors slammed shut behind them, Jinx sliding to the floor, pulling away from Ren to rip off his shirt. He did the same to her, removing her bra as his tongue flicked over her nipple. She held his head there, his hands pulling her closer to him.

Jinx pulled his head back, a wicked smile crossing her lips.

"Kneel." She ordered.

Ren did not object as he lowered himself to the ground before her, eyes glistening in anticipation. Her hand wrapped around his chin, angling his head up to her. She bent down slowly, brushing her lips lightly over his.

"I recall you telling me that you do not take orders." She smirked.

His hands traced up her legs, looking at her with a fire in his eyes. "I never had before."

"Tell me what you want." She breathed.

He groaned. "You."

Chuckling, she pulled away from him, finally realizing where she was. Ren's mountain escape.

She took her time, removing her boots, watching him as she did it. Once they were off, she pointed a finger to him, waving it towards her, signaling for him to come. He took no time in following the order, hands gripping her exposed upper half.

"Stand." She said.

He did, and she began a line of small pecks down his body. She continued lower, getting to his waist where she began to undo his pants. Jinx could feel the pleasure he hid beneath the fabric, being sure to brush over it as she slowly worked.

"You're evil." He groaned.

"That's the rumor." She smirked, pulling down his pants to reveal his pulsating manhood. "Oh." She said, the words escaping her. She hadn't realized how large he was. She never had anything so big before.

He chuckled, stepping out of his pants and lifting her in his arms. "I refuse for our first time to be in the entry of our home."

"Our home?" She asked.

He smirked, looking to her. "We aren't going to live with my parents forever."

Her eyes widened, Ren kicking open the door and tossing her onto the bed. He did not wait for an order before pulling off her leggings and placing a hand around her throat.

His knee was placed between her legs as he leaned forward, licking his lips. "You have no idea how long I've waited for this."

His hands spread her legs apart, lips grazing the inside of her thighs. She shuttered, waiting for him to take her in his mouth. Her breath became heavy, and finally he placed his lips over her, sucking and licking.

Jinx gasped, her hand grabbing onto his hair, eyes pinned on him. He watched her, seeing how she reacted to each move of his tongue and lips. After a series of flicks, Jinx closed her eyes, covering her mouth.

Ren pulled from her, his hand grabbing her wrist, uncovering her mouth. "I want to hear you scream."

Jinx's eyes shot open, watching as he hovered above her, his legs between hers.

"Say my name." He said with a dark smile. "Tell me you want me."

Jinx felt a heat cross over her as she remembered what he had told her when she had first come to Valder Manor.

"...never call me Mr. Valder unless you plan on me fucking you until you can't take anymore."

Her lips curled into a smile, lifting them to his. "Ruin me, Mr. Valder."

His eyes darkened as he thrust into her. Her hands wrapped around his neck, scratching along his back as she did, the ecstasy filling her. She hadn't realized how much she had craved him, how much her body wanted him inside of her.

"As you wish, Dorian."

His thrusts became faster, Jinx no longer able to hold back the moans of pleasure. His head lowered to her breast, tongue flicking over it as he continued pushing inside of her. She wrapped her legs around his waist, closing her eyes from the intensity.

Ren's hand firmly tugged her jaw, causing her to look to him. "If you close your eyes again, I'll stop. Understand?"

She nodded, his lips smashing against hers, tongues intertwining, her body locking to his.

"Fuck you feel so good." He moaned.

She smiled, biting the bottom of his lip. "I'm all you ever wanted." He moaned again, pleasure filling her. "All you'll ever need."

Jinx flipped him, just like training, his dick still hidden inside her. She pressed her hand against his neck, riding him as she looked down at his form beneath her.

Her legs burned as she pressed into him harder, her head tilting back as her climax built within her. She was jerked up, legs wrapping around him as Ren pressed her into the bookshelves along the wall, sending books falling around them.

He forced her hands over her head, lifting her leg to his shoulder as he continued to push himself inside of her. She screamed out, her body releasing into him. Ren only continued, sending her spiraling into another orgasm. Jinx's knee weakened, Ren letting her hands go and picking her leg up so he could continue. She wrapped her arms around his neck, his head leaning down to mark her. Claiming her in more ways than one.

Jinx came again and again, her body shaking as each orgasm filtered through her. Ren grinning wider with each tensing of her body.

"Say my name." He demanded.

"Fuck you." She laughed.

"God damn it Jinx, say my name."

"Come for me, Ren Valder."

Ren spun, slamming her back onto the bed, tensing as he released into her. He breathed heavily, sweat glistening over his body.

She took a finger, tilting his head up, her legs shaking. "Was it everything you dreamed of?"

He smiled, running his tongue over his teeth. "Everything and more."

"You know," Jinx smiled, biting her bottom lip, "I did say to ruin me, and I don't think you achieved that."

He laughed, his head falling to her chest. "If you can fucking walk right now, I will be more than happy to finish you off a few more times."

She ran her fingers through his hair, sighing deeply. "Let's test it."

Ren sucked on his teeth, rolling off of her, waving his hand to the floor. Books were scattered all throughout the room, Jinx not having a clue how one made it all the way to the door on the other side.

She took a deep breath, focusing on walking. Her legs shook as they hung off the side, Jinx pressing them to the ground, her leg giving out. Ren grabbed her before she fell, pulling her onto his lap.

"Well, Ms. Dorian, it looks as if, for the first time, you lost a challenge." Ren smirked, his eyes tracing the outline of her body.

"Mr. Valder, I object to these claims, seeing as I have managed to secure the entirety of your body and soul."

He chuckled. "You've secured more than that, Dorian."

Jinx shrieked a laugh as Ren tossed them to the bed.

She never wanted to leave that room or Ren's arms. He was completely devoted to her and her alone. And as she laid on that bed, with Ren's arm around her waist, his green eyes pinned to hers, she knew she was home.

Chapter Thirteen
The Necklace

Days went by quickly as Jinx and Ren entertained themselves as many new couples do. Though somethings did not change, such as their routine, only more vigorous activities were thrown into the mix.

Jinx had come out of the bedroom one morning, covered by a thin blanket over a large t-shirt. Her hair was in a random mix of curls and waves, causing Ren to do a double take as she entered the sitting area. Her coffee waited for her on the table, Ren laying across the bear skin rug, his head propped up by a pile of books.

"Teasing me so early in the morning, Dorian?" He chuckled.

Jinx smiled, dropping to the floor beside him, her leg lacing through his. "Is it really teasing if you always find me sexy?"

He lifted himself up, grabbing her chin and kissing her tenderly on the lips. "I have something for you."

Jinx perked up, hoping for a book on more magical plants having read all the others in the house. Ren lifted himself from the rug, feet smacking against the tiled floor towards the ballroom. When he had come back a small while after, he held a navy blue velvet box in his hand. It was easily the size of a book, though more square in shape.

She tilted her head to the side, watching as Ren sat on his knees in front of her, smiling down at the box. There was a soft layer of dust over the top, dimming the color.

"I've been saving this for you," He said, "A family heirloom that has been passed down through the generations."

Jinx smiled, biting her lip. "And you're giving it to me?"

Ren's green eyes sparkled as they looked to her. "One day, I would like to see you wearing this as you walk down the aisle." Her mouth dropped open causing him to chuckle. "I plan to live my life by your side Jinx, and that means marriage to me."

She nodded. Jinx had never expected to get married after being sorted as a Background Character. She never thought she could trust anyone to see the scars on her back, or the pain she had held within herself. But the way Ren talked about it, it's like he always knew she would be his wife, like he had been waiting for her to approve of him.

Ren opened the box, exposing the heirloom that rested inside.

It was marvelous.

A thick silver chain wrapped around a red velvet interior, attaching three metal plates. The outer plates were smaller, the size of her little finger's nail. Each held a blue gem at the ends, it glittering as the fire light flickered within it. The center plate was thicker, the size of her thumb. In the center a larger blue jewel rested, surrounding a crest. A sword piercing through a goblet, vines traveling around the sides, dipping down where a tear drop shape dripped from the goblet's bottom.

"It's the Valder family crest, and I want you to wear it. Think of it as a promise for our future, where you no longer will be a Dorian, but a Valder." Ren smiled.

A tear fell from Jinx's cheek, his hand reaching up to brush it away.

"Did I upset you?" He asked.

She shook her head, laughing. "No, I just, never thought I would have this. Have you."

He set the box on the coffee table, taking the necklace out and walking behind her. Jinx pulled her mess of hair to the side as Ren attached the clasp, letting the necklace hang around her. Her fingers grazed the cold metal, head looking up to him as he returned to his spot in front of her.

"Beautiful."

Jinx had a suspicion that he was not talking about the necklace, but about her, bed-head and all.

"You spoil me." She teased.

"I was under the impression you enjoyed being pampered Ms. Dorian."

She clicked her tongue, looking to the side. "I guess it could be worse." She faked a sigh.

Ren took his place on the floor beside her, Jinx wrapping herself into him again. Her smile faded as she remembered why they were living there in the first place.

"How long until you have to go back?" She asked, her fingers grazing the buttons on his shirt.

He sighed, leaning his head back. "Soon. I have a bone to pick with Micha, especially now."

Jinx shook her head. "Thaddeus will be working with him, you can't defeat both of them."

"I can't let you come with, Jinx." He scoffed.

She moved over him, sitting on his lap, facing him. "Like it or not, I am a Villain now too. Just as you have your responsibility to Micha, I have one to Thaddeus."

"And what if you get hurt, or worse yet, killed?" He grumbled darkly. "What am I supposed to do then?"

She placed both hands on his face, forcing him to look at her. "Stop thinking about me dying. We live in a world where either of us could be killed due to a stupid separation a machine decided. If we are partners, our worlds won't have to be so difficult."

"You were much easier to manage when you were Morally Gray." Ren muttered.

"I was also much easier to kill." Jinx said angrily. "I have something to fight for Ren. I want this and I want you, don't feel like you must do it alone."

Ren's hand went to the back of her neck, their foreheads pressing together.

"You have done so much for me, don't try to stop me from helping you this time." She whispered.

He sighed, his arms wrapping around her and his head resting on her shoulder. She wrapped her arms over his shoulders, a hand gliding through his hair.

"We're safer together." She whispered.

"Unstoppable." Ren chuckled into her.

"The most powerful Villain duo to grace the streets of Central City." She teased.

"Do you really think you can take on Thaddeus?" Ren asked, pulling back. "Can you kill your own brother?"

Jinx clenched her teeth together, looking to the fire with a frown. The flames reflected in her eyes, displaying the hatred within them.

"Thaddeus is not my brother. He lost that right when he had helped Packard torture me." Jinx shook her head, sucking on her teeth. "I could kill him without so much as blinking."

Ren smirked. "That's my girl."

She sighed, leaning her head against his chest. "What happens when they die?"

Ren kissed the top of her head. "Mom said it was like a relief. She said she was bored because she was always fighting her Hero, and then she didn't have to."

"Packard will come for us when we kill Thaddeus and Micha."

Ren nodded. "My dad is prepared for that."

He laid down, Jinx resting comfortably on his chest as he played with her hair. She closed her eyes listening to every beat of his heart like it would be the last time she ever heard it. She was scared to lose him, to find that he was gone and she would be alone again. Jinx knew that if anything happened to Ren, no Hero would be able to stop her from destroying Central City and Honorville.

"I love you." She said quietly, a tear slipping from her.

"I love you." He whispered. "But let's not spend the next few days stressing about what tomorrow brings. I personally would love if you would model for me."

"Model?" Jinx asked, raising an eyebrow as she lifted herself to look at him.

"First outfit, nothing but that necklace around your neck." He smirked.

She closed her eyes, shaking her head with a smile. "Ren Valder are you still not tired after we fucked everywhere in this estate?"

He lifted himself to her, their faces inches apart as he cupped her cheek. "My dear, we will have to have sex at least a thousand times in every inch of this house for me to ever feel like I've had enough."

She smiled, looking to his lips then back to his eyes. "That is a very high goal. May take us our entire lives."

"What. A. Pity." Ren said as he pushed Jinx to the ground with a kiss.

Two bodies, one soul, and the motivation to kill everyone they cross paths with if they are separated. A true love match.

Chapter Fourteen
Alter Ego

Ren was very slow to introduce Jinx into baths again. He had made sure to have a large tub in their home, not for adjusting her to the water, but for other reasons he had planned before he had saved her.

While Ren claimed it was a tub, Jinx related it more to a small pool. She would've easily swum laps in it as a kid, the water refilling from a collection that rained down from the jagged rock ceiling of the mountain. Bubbles filled the edges of the water, something that Jinx found relaxed her slightly. The white tiles beneath her feet were always warm as she walked across them, having a sneaking suspicion that Ren made sure the floor was heated. A closet door was off to the side, made from a crystal structure that sparkled in the minimal light of the small windows past the bath.

Ren had lowered himself into the water first, offering his hand to Jinx. She clutched onto the large bathrobe, trying to stop her shaking hands. She could do this, if she just pushed through, she could get over this fear that consumed her.

She dropped the robe around her, closing her eyes as she took Ren's hand, allowing him to lead her in. Jinx felt her body scream in protest of her being in the water, her hand tightening against his.

"You're doing great." His voice soothed.

She nodded, peaking at him as she was able to get waist deep.

Jinx took deep breaths, Ren smiling at her for the progress. While she did not have the major anxiety attack she had the first few times, her stomach still knotted and her head felt light.

"Lots of progress this week," Ren said, "My dear, you prove to me just how strong you are every day."

"Cut the sweet talk, Ren, I'm fucking shaking because I'm so scared." She snapped.

He nodded. "Yes, but you got further than you did yesterday."

"I still won't be able to do it alone anytime soon." She huffed.

Ren smirked. "Good."

Jinx laughed nervously, slowly squatting down as the water rose up her body. "Taking advantage of my trauma is not going to get you more sex."

"No, and it does make my heart ache seeing you this way, but," He moved closer to her kissing her forehead, "I spent too long apart from you to not take advantage of spending all the time I can with you."

Jinx rolled her eyes, smirking. "Come now Mr. Valder, you can't say things like that if you were never apart from me."

Ren sighed dramatically. "See, in my books, the stalking didn't count."

Jinx laughed, wrapping her arms around his neck. When he was there, everything was okay. There was no pain or challenges that she would have to face alone, only inconveniences.

"We can't spend all day in here," Ren said pitifully, "My mother is coming over."

"Meg? Why?"

"You're a Villain, Jinx, you cannot cause havoc in a sweater and leggings." Ren laughed.

Jinx pursed her lips. "I definitely could."

"I mean, yes, you could, but where's the fun in that?"

Jinx nodded, though she wasn't sure exactly what type of Villain apparel she would want to wear. It was like a costume, something to conceal her identity, but everyone already knew who she was. Jinx Dorian, three-time sorted daughter of Heroes, turned Villain. She was all over the news.

She thought back to the other Villains she had seen. Knox had worn a long black cape and a mask that covered his entire face. The suit was leather looking, leaving everything covered except for his hands, where his power came from. Meg wore a white dress that was never cleaned from the blood that splattered onto it, causing many to fear her. Ren wore his black suit and masquerade mask, which she did like, though did not want anyone calling her a clown like Micha had done to him.

"I think I have an idea," She said, "It's a bit different."

"I'm sure it'll look marvelous." He smiled.

Meg had arrived a little after noon. She was followed by two Henchmen wearing masks sewn like a scarecrow. Jinx shook off the strange feeling she got from it as Meg led her into an office off the sitting room.

"Jinx, I am so excited to be able to do this with you," Meg exclaimed as the scarecrow Henchmen started to unpack bags. "I loved doing this with Ren, but it's not the same with a boy and the only other girl I helped had no imagination save for her glasses she chose."

Jinx chuckled, pulling out a sketchbook she had been drawing her idea in. "Now, I know it isn't great, I'm no artist, but this is sort of what I was thinking."

Meg took the notebook from her hand, eyes lighting up as she looked over the pages.

"The corset, is it-."

"Lined with body armor." Jinx said.

"And the pants?"

"Black spandex with a leather pattern."

Meg's smile grew as she looked over the drawing, Jinx feeling more validated as she watched the woman.

"What color red?" Meg asked waving a hand to a Henchman who brought over colored patches.

Jinx flipped through each one, stopping at a dark maroon. She smiled. "I want this, but I want lace embroidered around the edges, especially the bottom."

"What if, instead of lace, we do a custom embroidery?" Meg asked with her brows raised.

"What did you have in mind?" Jinx asked.

Meg fingered the necklace around Jinx's throat, looking at it lovingly. "Our family crest, laced into the fabric in a gold color. You are one of us now, especially since the things your father said."

Jinx furrowed her brows. "What did my father say?"

Meg cocked her head to the side, removing her hand from the necklace and placing it on her hip. "Have you not seen the press release?"

Jinx shook her head.

Meg walked to the desk, getting a remote and pushing a button. The television on the far wall turned on, Meg switching it to the channel with ongoing coverage of Villains and Heroes.

Packard, Olivia, Thaddeus, and Micha all stood on a podium; multiple microphones pointed to them.

"As many of you know, my daughter, Jinx Dorian, has been sorted as a Villain. She had hurt our family dearly, even going as far as to place myself and Micha into a comatose state." Packard stated.

"Yeah, after he almost beat me to death." Jinx hissed.

"What you don't know, is that Jinx is not biologically my daughter."

Jinx stopped, her eyes widening and mouth parting open.

"I had found her when she was just a baby on the boarder of Vileterra. I had brought her into my home, since we had just lost a child of our own."

"That's not true! My mother has pictures of me and a birth certificate with *my* name!" Jinx exclaimed.

"Jinx Dorian is not a Dorian, but from the Ursu family."

Jinx slouched, leaning back against the desk with her arms crossed. Her jaw tightened, her head shaking as she realized what he was doing. Packard was saving the family name. Not only did he disown her, but he placed a Villain family name onto her that had been wiped out long ago.

"Central City will believe him." Meg said with a harshness to her tone. "They always believe the Heroes."

"Ren knows my sizes, get the measurements from him." Jinx growled, rushing out of the room and down the hall towards their bedroom.

"Jinx?" Ren called out, but she ignored him.

She kicked open the door, the force taking the entire door off the wall, it sliding across the room. She marched to the bookshelf, her finger scanning over the books angrily until she landed on the one she was looking for.

Villain Family Trees

She flipped through the pages, scanning the tops for the Ursu family lineage. She found it, looking at the names listed along the side.

Fenri Ursu – Brown hair, gray eyes, magic shielding.

Lottie Ursu – Brown hair, green eyes, magic manipulation.

Tenson Ursu – Black hair, blue eyes, magic detection.

Elias Ursu – brown hair, gray eyes, magic absorption.

Jinx furrowed her brows, looking at the last entry.

Unknown Ursu – Brown hair, gray eyes, last of family line-powers unknown.

Jinx slammed the book shut, her body shaking in anger. Was it possible she had come from the Ursu family line? Her gray eyes and brown hair didn't fit in with her mother or father's, her brother did not have any of her physical traits either.

It was then that everything clicked.

"Jinx?" Ren said warily by the doorway.

"I was never a fucking Dorian. It was why I was targeted." She said turning to him. "My brown hair, my eyes, they aren't Dorian traits, they're Ursu traits. It makes sense why I was tortured my entire life and Thaddeus was never harmed. They were terrified I would become a Villain like my family lineage suggested, so they tried to beat it out of me."

Ren furrowed his brows. "What are you talking about?"

"Packard disowned me in a press conference, Ren. He claimed I was not his child, but found on the Vileterra border. He says I'm an Ursu, and it makes sense!"

Ren walked over the door on the floor, sitting on the side of the bed. "Ursu? Like Elias Ursu?"

Jinx nodded. "That was the last Ursu to have been a Villain, killed by-."

"Your mother." Ren said, running his hand through his hair. "It was major because she was only a Love Interest, killing a high-level Villain-."

"And then suddenly, there was me."

"Holy fuck." Ren whispered. "Holy fuck you're the last surviving Ursu."

Jinx shook her head. "We don't know for sure, but I would like to get it tested eventually. For now, we know that I am able to block magical attacks and detect it. Thaddeus is able to absorb it, so what if we see what else I can do?"

"Do you think you can do more?" Ren asked.

Jinx walked to him, straddling his lap. Her hands wrapped around his neck as she smiled. "If I'm the last surviving Ursu, then why not have all the powers of my ancestors?"

Ren laughed. "I love your enthusiasm, but I come from a long line of people was multiple powers and I only got teleportation and minor magic."

Jinx clicked her tongue. "That's because you suck and I'm brilliant."

Ren laughed, throwing her onto the bed, rolling on top of her. "And to think I've been calling you Dorian all this time."

"From an outsider perspective, you need to work on your stalking skills." Jinx teased.

"I'll never be perfect, as unfortunate as that is." He chuckled, leaning down to kiss her neck.

"If you were, I don't think things between us would work." She sighed.

"How do you suspect?"

She grabbed his hair, pulling his head back so he looked into her eyes. "How could I love all of you when there are no imperfections to love?"

"I mean, I would be perfect, but possibly a wonky nose." He chuckled.

"Fuck off." Jinx laughed, pulling his head down to kiss her.

He pulled away, smiling at her. "What do you think of kids?"

She raised her eyebrows, sucking in her lips. "I would like them one day, just after everything settles down and we don't have Heroes to torture."

Ren nodded, giving her quick pecks over her face. "I want a daughter, with your eyes and my hair."

"Pretty cocky not giving her mine." Jinx sighed.

Ren traveled his lips across her jaw. "Fine we can have two girls one with my eyes and your hair."

"Deal." Jinx breathed as Ren's lips trailed down to her collarbones. "But I want a son."

"A boy?" He asked, stopping to look up to her.

"Did I tell you to stop?" She smirked.

"My apologies." Ren said, continuing to kiss lower.

"I want a boy with your hair and each of our eyes."

Ren lifted Jinx's shirt, lips closing tenderly over her raised nipple. "Awfully picky for our son."

Jinx shuttered, her legs wrapping around Ren's waist. "You promised you'd give me anything I wanted."

His hands traced up her legs, lifting the skirt she had decided to wear that day. "Unfortunately, I am not a god. Somethings are just out of my capabilities." His fingers circled her clit, spreading the lips for better access.

"Stop teasing me Ren." Jinx whispered.

"Oh, but do I love the way I make you squirm."

His fingers dived into her, Jinx gasping as they flicked inside. Her legs came up, Ren positioning his shoulders beneath them as he continued to play with her.

"Your mom-." Jinx moaned, forgetting Meg had been in her home moments earlier.

"Left." Ren confirmed.

He kept his fingers inside of her, thrusting them in and out as he removed his pants with the other hand. Jinx clenched the sheets of the bed in her hands, arching her back reflectively.

"Say it." He growled, rubbing his erect cock.

Instead, Jinx untangled her legs from him, sliding to the floor in front of him. She looked up, opening her mouth. Her lips slowly slid over his manhood, her tongue flicking over the tip, enjoying the pulsing it caused. He grabbed onto her hair, encouraging her to go deeper.

"Get on the bed." He ordered.

Jinx removed her mouth from him, Ren not waiting for her to stand before he bent down, tossing her onto the mattress. He paused, gazing at her.

She smirked, raising an eyebrow as she slowly spread her legs apart, her fingers rubbing over her clit. "What's the matter, Valder, scared you'll break me?"

"No," He growled, "I'm scared you'll break me."

She bit her lip. "Let's find out."

He pounced onto the bed, his hand around her throat and the other resting on her waist. His hips thrust forward, his cock finding its way into her. She moaned loudly, Ren grinning wide.

"Do it again." He whispered, thrusting into her. "Do it so loud they hear it in Honorville."

He pushed into her faster and harder than he had before, his eyes pinned on her, watching the expressions that contorted on her face. She screamed, head arching back as she felt the power of her orgasm build inside of her.

"I'm going to come." She moaned.

"No you won't." He smiled viciously. "You will come when I tell you to."

"Ren!" Jinx protested, but he only thrust into her faster.

"Please." She begged.

"No." He growled.

She tried to hold it, the feeling intensifying as she gripped his arms. "Please."

He was silent, Jinx feeling she would burst any second.

"Come for me."

She released, a wave of euphoria crashing over her, curling her toes into the mattress. Ren didn't wait for her to finish, flipping her over and grabbing her shoulder as he continued ramming into her.

It went deeper than before, his dick pressing into her so rough, but it felt wonderful. She rocked her hips in motion with his thrusts, causing him to release a groan. Jinx looked back to him with a smile, his eyes glistening as they met hers.

"That the best you got?" She teased.

He laughed, removing himself from her. He grabbed her ankle, pulling her towards him. She yelped as he lifted her over his shoulder like she weighed nothing and exited their room. He walked down the hall and flung the door open to the ballroom, the colors dancing over the floor.

He walked up the few steps to the piano, sitting her on top of it as he lowered himself between her legs. His tongue danced over her, circling her clit expertly. Her legs wrapped around his shoulders, thighs clenching as he sucked on her. The keys played an uncoordinated song as she moved, filling the room with sounds of her pleasure and the badly placed notes. Another wave of pleasure built within her, breaths shaking as it came to a climax.

"Ren." She whimpered.

"Not yet." He said between a flicking tongue.

She squeaked her discomfort, Ren sucking on her intensely.

"I can't-." She moaned as she came again.

Ren pulled away, standing, his hand gripping her throat. "Did I tell you to come?"

"No, but-."

He grabbed her, sliding her off the piano and spinning her around. She gripped the wood where she had been sitting as Ren slid inside of her.

Jinx screamed as he pounded into her, filling her with euphoria. He laughed as she did, building the orgasms that came one after another. Ren relished in each tightening of her body, his hands gripping her waist so she could not escape from him.

"Are you ready for me?" He grunted.

"Wait." Jinx ordered breathlessly. "I want to come one more time first."

"Jinx-." He grumbled.

"I said wait."

Ren groaned as he thrust into her, his hand sliding between her thighs, trying to stimulate her more. As the orgasm grew, she held it back, smiling as she watched Ren's jaw tighten from the strain. She released, calling out loudly so the sound echoed around the ballroom. Ren moaned, his body stiffening against her.

"Good boy." She giggled.

"I fucking hate you." He laughed.

"No you don't."

He twisted her around, a hand clutching her back while the other grabbed the nape of her neck. He pressed his lips into hers, her hands wrapping around him, intensifying the kiss.

"I could marry you right now." He said.

Jinx pursed her lips. "I expect a better proposal than this."

Ren laughed, shaking his head. "You should know by now that I go above and beyond for you."

She cocked her head to the side. "You gave me your heirloom necklace when I was wearing nothing but your shirt and a blanket."

"Oh, I'm sorry would you like me to take it back and redo it?" He teased reaching for the necklace at her throat.

She grabbed his wrist narrowing her eyes. "I will cut your hand off if you try and take it."

Ren looked her up and down, licking his lips. "I need ten minutes before you try to go seducing me like that."

She threw his hand to the side, walking past him with an extra swing in her hips.

"Again with the seduction!" He called after her.

She raised both hands, middle fingers lifted in the air as she left the room. All she heard as she left was Ren's low chuckle.

Chapter Fifteen
A Night on the Town

It only took a day for Meg to come back with her suit. Presented to her in a black box with a red bow, fitting for the color scheme she chose.

Meg sat on the arm of a chair, her hand on Knox. Ren sat in a chair opposite his parents, all looking at her, excited to see what she thought of her own design.

Jinx placed both hands flat on the box, smiling to them. "I want to show you all, not just lay out the outfit."

"Well please do!" Knox exclaimed, clapping his hands.

Jinx had never been so accepted before and the excitement that Knox and Meg showed her was something she had wished from her own family.

She hurried to the room, the box in hand. While the door had been reattached, the room was destroyed. One bookcase laid on its side, books piled on the floor below it. There were no sheets or blankets properly on the bed, all waterfalling off the side. Feathers littered the ground from a pillow that had exploded in a pillow fight that had happened earlier that morning.

She set the box down on the bed, removing the ribbon and lifting the lid. A wide smile spread over her face as she looked down to see the mask she requested, made perfectly to match her drawing.

Jinx placed each part onto the bed, starting with her under suit, she found the spandex conforming to her curves, not at all uncomfortable. The neckline fell low towards her breasts, the bottom being covered by an under bust corset that sinched around her waist. She placed the elbow length gloves over her fingers, then added the coat. It was even better than she had thought. The maroon coat stretched down to the floor, the seams having a looping black design similar to the crest she wore around her neck. It looked much better than the gold that Meg had suggested, and she was glad it was changed.

Pulling her hair into a ponytail, Jinx pulled the black mask over her head. Looking in the mirror, it made the whole outfit come together. The mask was similar to Ren's as it only covered her eyes, but instead of stopping there, it moved up over her hairline. Pointed arches danced over her head, like a crown. It was perfect.

"Ren, can you get me a gun belt?" She called out.

She waited a few minutes, the door opening but she hid behind it, giggling. "You can't look yet."

"Is it bad luck?" He chuckled handing her a black belt through the crack.

"No, but I want the look finished."

"As you wish." He said, closing the door behind him.

She fastened the black leather belt over her waist, attaching the curved holsters to her thighs. Finally, she pulled on the tall, black leather boots, fastening them up using the stiff ties.

She stared at herself in the mirror, smirking. She looked evil.

Opening the door, she heard the voices stop. Jinx walked with confidence into the sitting room, her lips, having been painted red, smiling.

"Holy hell." Knox muttered.

"Holy hell, indeed." Meg nodded, her mouth having fallen open.

Ren did not say anything, his hand covering his lower face as his eyes traced up and down her body.

Jinx looked down, furrowing her brows. "I thought it looked good, is there something wrong with it?"

"No, darling, it's just, well-." Meg started.

"It's hot." Ren said, his voice husky.

Jinx began to laugh, it increased with each passing second. She clutched her stomach, bending over from the stupidity of the situation.

"That's my real superpower," She cackled, "Being devastatingly attractive."

Meg put some fingers to her lips, looking from Jinx as she too chuckled. Knox put a hand on his wife's leg, smiling widely at Jinx.

"With a laugh like that, the entirety of Central City will be nervous." He said.

"How so?" Jinx asked, moving to lean against the fireplace.

Knox's eyes glimmered as he remembered the past. "You sound unhinged."

Her eyes glowed with the words, looking to Ren for confirmation.

Ren nodded. "It made even me nervous."

"Now you need a Villain name." Meg smiled, "Though, the people will give you that."

Jinx clicked her tongue. "As long as it isn't 'Clown' I think it'll be fine."

Ren fell back in his chair, groaning. "It's not even a clown, it's a god damned jester mask. I swear I got paired with the most dumbass Hero there is."

"Sore subject?" Jinx teased, spitting out her bottom lip.

Ren cocked his head, raising his eyebrows at her. "You want to test me woman?"

Jinx walked to him, sitting on the arm of his chair. "Darling, do behave, we have guests."

"I could murder you." He grumbled, sighing deeply.

Jinx smirked. "Kinky."

Meg and Knox stood, Jinx looking to them confused. "As much as we adore seeing you both, we have some—business to attend to." Meg smirked to Knox.

"Ugh, Mom." Ren groaned, placing his hands over his eyes.

Jinx giggled, watching as the two walked towards the door, a yellow shimmering light encompassing them, and they vanished.

"You know," Jinx said as she slid into Ren's lap, "I would love to see you in your suit." She trailed her fingers up his shirt.

His eyebrows raised, lips pursing. "Would you now?"

"I am all dolled up, you might as well be too." Jinx said slyly.

"Give me five minutes." Ren smiled, a glint to his eye.

He moved Jinx to the side of the chair and jogged to their room. She laughed as she watched him, knowing this would not be the last time they would be masked for each other.

Jinx was still picking feathers out of her hair as she sat on the counter of their kitchen. Ren tossed a caesar salad, listening to the news as Jinx nibbled on a stick of celery.

"You know, they really should just ignore the library fee for late books, it's not very practical." She commented after seeing the segment on the Central City Public Library. "Actually, I think I may have a book or two in my old apartment very overdue."

"I returned them the day after I rescued you." He said casually.

Jinx raised her eyebrows. "What an un-villainly move of you."

He shrugged. "I already had those books, so why would I need them?"

She pointed the celery stick at him smiling. "Touché."

"Go sit down, Princess, I'm almost finished here."

"Princess, huh?" She giggled as she jumped off the counter.

Ren looked to her. "What, you don't like it?"

Jinx shook her head as she slid into the wooden chair of the small kitchen table. "It's just not as good as Dorian."

"I can't keep calling you Dorian now can I?" He chuckled.

"I guess not," Jinx sighed dramatically, "You know what I wouldn't mind being called though?"

He raised his eyebrows, the corner of his lips lifting. "And what would that be?"

"Valder."

Ren stopped mixing the salad, letting go of the mixers and planted his hands onto the island counter. He hung his head down, black hair falling over his face.

"You test me every day." He muttered, a strain in his voice.

Jinx's fingers found the necklace, toying with it as she waited for him to recover. She knew he had been wanting to call her that, it was why he adored her calling him Mr. Valder, implying there was a Mrs.

"I'm not joking Ren, you're my only family now, it only fits." She said as he brought two plates to the table. Jinx cut into a piece of chicken, the food, as always, delicious. She smiled, humming her satisfaction.

He smirked, cutting into his own meal. "I want to give you a wedding and do everything you want."

"See, I was raised a Hero, as I'm sure you know." She said through a mouthful of food. "I want to do everything opposite now. Let me have my rebellious phase."

He set down his fork and knife, placing his arms on the table. "And what would be the rebellious alternative to getting a wedding Jinx?"

She smiled. "Forcing the courts to recognize us as married."

His eyes lit up at the idea, his green aura glowing around him. "What do you have in mind?"

"Well, we get our suits on, your mom already gave me the paperwork, so that's done, and we force them to marry us, right in front of that big, fancy, indoor fountain city hall has."

Ren placed a hand to his cheek, looking at her lovingly. "I should have kidnapped you sooner."

"Then marry me sooner." Jinx grinned.

"Mrs. Jinx Valder," He hummed, "I like the sound of that."

"Now imagine moaning it."

Ren's eyes widened as he stood from the table. He grabbed her hand, pulling her out of her seat, and towards the bedroom. "Get your suit on, we're storming city hall."

Jinx was carried wedding style as Ren teleported them to the steps of city hall. Citizens of Central City moved out of the way quickly, especially after seeing Jinx's crazed smile.

Ren had hired several Henchmen to clear their way, two opening the doors wide for them to enter. Jinx raised up her hand-held machine gun, shooting into the ceiling.

"Attention citizens of Central City!" Jinx announced, slipping from Ren's grasp. "Someone fucking marry us, and no one will die… right away."

She looked to Ren, who reading her face said, "Sounding good."

This whole Villain thing was unusual, but she decided to embrace the anger and manic side of her while wearing the uniform. It wasn't the same person she was in the mountain side home with Ren, but someone more primal from within her.

Being a Background Character in the past, Jinx had found the judge's office quick, often delivering money to him when the city hall requested it. Kicking open the door, with Ren and three Henchmen behind her, Jinx's eyes glistened as she caught him, pants down, being sucked off by a Background Character.

"Mr. Judge, what would your wife say if she saw you now?" Jinx's finger waving disapprovingly, enjoying the panicked look he had while trying to pull up his pants.

Jinx bounced over to the desk, spreading the other papers and ornaments off it, sitting and spinning cross legged to face him. Her smile grew as Ren's hand slid around her waist, she could practically feel his excitement.

"What do you want?" The judge hissed as the Background Character rushed from the room.

"We've got these papers here. Sign them." Ren growled, his smile unwavering sending a butterflied explosion through Jinx.

"And if I don't?" He hissed.

Jinx held up a semi-automatic pistol in her hand, having given the machine gun to a Henchman to hold. The gun was engraved with a mask, like the one Ren wore, making it one of her favorites. That, and the recoil was not awful.

The judge looked between the barrel pointed between his eyes and her smiling face, head cocked to the side. "Now I don't think you're stupid enough to deny a simple request."

He shook his head, picking a pen up, and looked over the paperwork. His brows furrowed, head jerking back in shock. "This is a marriage license for Ren Valder and-."

"Jinx Dorian, at your disservice." She sang. "Now sign the fucking things. I want to be rid of that ugly family name."

The judge nodded, brows slick with the beads of sweat that formed from his stress. The pen glided over the papers quickly, Ren, getting bored, began to twirl Jinx's ponytail, sending shivers down her spine.

"If you don't stop, I will take you here in front of everyone." She giggled, her head moving back towards him, eyes never leaving the judge.

"Is that a promise, Valder?" Ren said, eyes sparkling.

Jinx bit her lip. "If you want it to be."

"I'm done." The judge huffed, looking between the two Villains nervously.

Ren took the papers, looking through them with a grin. "You're officially Mrs. Valder."

Jinx smiled brightly, hoping off the desk. Ren handed the papers to a Henchman, ordering to have him file it. As the Henchman took off, Ren placed a gloved hand around her throat, another pulling her waist to him. His lips pressed against hers, her tongue slowly sneaking into his mouth. A kiss of pure ecstasy.

Her hands went to his head, gun still present in one of them. When he finally pulled from her, there was a look he gave her, one that melted her to the core.

"I have a surprise for you." He said.

"I love your surprises." She giggled.

"Follow me." Ren took her hand, walking out of the judge's room. Before they left, Jinx raised the gun, pulling the trigger. A bullet shot through the judge's head, a perfect hit right between the eyes. His body slumped forward onto the wooden desk as Ren gave her a raised eyebrow.

"I couldn't let him get away with cheating on our wedding day. It has to be bad luck." She said with a pout.

Ren grinned, lifting her in his arms. "How could I have been so oblivious to not remember that?" He teased.

He set Jinx in front of a fountain, the water now dyed red, the traditionally white marble spray painted black with "Valder" over the sides.

"You all have been witnessed to a monumental day in Villain history!" Ren announced. "May I introduce my wife, previously Ms. Jinx Dorian, now Mrs. Jinx Valder." He leaned down towards her, smile growing. "The Villain Queen."

"Ren, did you just give me my Villain alter-ego?" Jinx asked.

"Do you not like it? With the mask, it looked like a crown in my mind." He said casually.

"Quite the opposite, I love it!" She shrieked as Ren spun her around, holding her back as he leaned down and kissed her. He trailed the kisses up her arm and to her hand.

He looked to the people staring with wide eyes, his smile dropping. "Kneel for your fucking Queen."

The people began to kneel, others who stayed standing were confronted by the Henchmen, who forced them to their knees. To either side of her, sparkling fireworks went off, and explosions sounded off in the distance.

She gasped, looking to him. "Ren, what did you blow up?"

"I started with the remains of the bank, of course, then the bridge from Central City to Honorville. Oh, and then the school."

"You blew up the school?" She asked excitedly.

"All the places I waited for you and couldn't have you. I don't have that issue any longer, so no need to have those places." He smirked.

She laughed as he swung her to the side. "You're such a romantic."

"Anything to make you smile." He said.

"Anything?"

"Don't make me repeat myself, Valder."

There was a commotion by the doors, Henchmen flying from them as Thaddeus, in an awful green spandex suit, and Micha, in his blue and white one, entered.

"Wedding crashers." Jinx pouted.

"They never do have good timing." Ren agreed.

"Leave these people alone, Clown." Micha yelled.

Jinx rolled her eyes, placing a hand on her hip. "Micha, do some fucking research, he's not a clown, it's a jester mask. You're making yourself look stupid."

Micha opened and closed his mouth, unsure of how to respond to verbal assaults.

"Jinx, you look well." Thaddeus snarled, "Though you'd look better without the Villain get up."

Ren's arm wrapped around Jinx's shoulders. "Funny, isn't it, Thaddeus, how you expected her to come out a Hero after beating her so brutally she almost died?" Thaddeus went white, eyes looking to Micha.

"Aren't Heroes supposed to protect the people, especially seeing as I was only a child when our father began my whipping?" Jinx cocked her head to the side with a snide smile on her lips.

The people kneeling looked between the Heroes and Villains with confusion. This was what Jinx wanted, to switch the narrative in her favor. She had noticed the reporter in city hall when she had arrived, his recorder blinking red, having been on the entire time.

"But according to Packard Dorian, I was never his child to begin with, was I?" Jinx smirked, "An Ursu, is what he claims. A Hero who took in a Villain child, only to try and beat the Villainy out of her. Tragic it only helped me get here."

"Dad only did what was best for us." Thaddeus objected.

Jinx grinned maliciously. "Is that why you don't have any scars, Thad? Why you always turned up the music when my screams ran throughout the house?"

Thaddeus shifted, uncomfortable, the people staring at both of them in horror.

"You broke the treaty to kidnap me when I was perfectly happy." Jinx snapped, her smile turning into a snarl. "You took me to that torture cabin and hung me from that tree until my arms dislocated and shoulder blades protruded from inside my body." Ren's eyes got wide, listening to her list out the tortures they had put her through, never having talked about it yet. "And then the drowning. I still can't handle baths from that, you know. The very sound of water splashing had sent me into a panic." Her eyes narrowed. "You don't drown your sister, Thaddeus."

The people kneeling were no longer looking to the Villains, but to the Heroes with horrified glances. Jinx had convinced them, with a few words and emotion in her voice that the Heroes had been the bad guys. This small group of people witnessing her wedding, realized why Jinx was a Villain now.

"This is your fault." Thaddeus pulled out two throwing knives, launching them towards Ren. Without thinking, Jinx stepped in front of Ren as the two knives were about to hit, a glowing blue bubble surrounding them.

The knives bounced off the bubble, clattering on the floor loudly.

"I guess it wasn't just magic after all." Ren whispered. "But if you try to do something like that again, I will never forgive you."

"Bite me." Jinx snapped back. She pulled out her pistols, pointing one at Micha and one at Thaddeus, walking forward. Jinx had a new hatred in her eyes. They tried to kill her, she could accept that, but trying to kill Ren? That was something worthy of a death penalty. She fired off the guns, bullets hitting both men and simply bouncing off.

"Micha is resistant to bullets and is strong." Ren called to her with a smile.

"Could've told me that sooner." She huffed.

Ren winked to her, teleporting behind Micha and punched him in the side of the head. Jinx went to Thaddeus, smirking.

"Just like old times, brother." She hissed.

He snarled, pulling out a sword. A boring weapon to choose in the world of firearms. She ran at him, Thaddeus slicing sideways across the air, Jinx sliding between his legs and retrieving the other sword he had in his frog. He turned, seeing her with the Dorian crested sword.

"What would father have said?" She faked a gasp.

Thaddeus came out her, their swords clashing in a series of sharp tangs throughout the building. They were trained equally, however, Packard Dorian had taught Jinx that failure comes with a price. One lesson she was not privy to ignore.

Jinx saw it as a dance of sorts. While powerful and dangerous, she could easily see the next move Thaddeus was to make. He swung towards her head, her sword reaching up to block the attack, pushing back against his. She spun, going for his side, his sword meeting hers, though, it was unstable.

She smiled, knowing where Thaddeus was weak. She began a series of assaults in a traditional order her father had trained them. Left, right, down, up. Repeating the pattern until Thaddeus moved his sword with her. That's when she hit. Left, right, left.

She sliced the hand his sword resided in, causing him to drop it. In a few quick steps, she managed to kick the sword further, slicing at his chest, opening the spandex suit. She spun, the sword cutting into his side and Jinx pulling it towards her. He looked to her with wide eyes, his hand covering the wound. Thaddeus fell to his knees, Jinx kicking the sword from his hand as she knelt over him.

"You've always underestimated me," She hissed, "Today, that was your downfall."

She sliced the blade across his throat, blood splattering over her exposed skin. Thaddeus' eyes rolled back, his head barely hanging onto his neck.

Jinx stood from him, turning to see Micha and Ren still fighting. She strut over to them, an angry smile on her face, amplified by the blood of her brother. Ren peaked to her, a malicious smile clearly present. His lip was split, a small amount of his own blood over his chin. His slicked hair was not a touch out of place, but he did have several red marks where bruises would surely form.

"Oh shit." Ren chuckled, causing Micha to look at her.

His jaw dropped open as he watched Jinx come at him, sword dragging on the ground.

"Do you think I would just let you ruin my wedding day and get away with it?" She laughed manically, her eyes widening. "Not to mention the torture you helped with."

Micha backed away from the two Villains, fingering his belt for any weapon to use.

"Scared Micha?" Ren hissed excitedly. "Were you this scared when you took your turn whipping my defenseless wife?"

"I-I had to do it, Packard he-."

Jinx put a sword to his throat, clicking her tongue as she watched his Adam's apple bob. She looked to Ren from the corner of her eyes, fluttering them.

"He is your Hero." She smiled.

Ren sighed, shaking his head and smiling. "You give me such lovely gifts."

"Ren, wait! I'll stop calling you a clown, I don't want to-." Micha pleaded, but Jinx pressed the sword closer to his throat.

Ren furrowed his brows. "You just don't get it, Micha. I would love for you to keep living your life, but I am bored with being your Villain."

Ren took several steps forward, his eyes darkening, the green almost completely absorbed in black. "I've been practicing this for what you did to Mrs. Valder."

He placed his hands to Micha's temples. Micha's eyes were immediately consumed in a flash of red, his nose and mouth producing the same light. His skin slowly melted away, leaving a brown, burning skeleton where Micha once stood.

Jinx pulled the sword away as Ren stepped back, his arm wrapping around her shoulders. They watched Micha's body burn the rest of the way, his skeleton crumbling into a pile of ash.

"You could do that the entire time?" Jinx asked, shocked.

Ren chuckled. "Just some minor magic."

"That's minor? You burned him alive!" She exclaimed.

He shrugged. "He deserved it."

Ren's hand went to Jinx's cheek cupping it there. She leaned into it, smiling softly and closing her eyes. "We don't have any Heroes anymore."

"Yes, it was interesting how fast you managed to kill Thaddeus." Ren commented.

Jinx looked to him. "Thaddeus never excelled in sword fighting, he only liked using them as a weapon to look cool. I, on the other hand, was forced to be proficient in all manners of weapons."

Ren laughed, kissing her on the forehead. "Come on, let's go."

Jinx clung tightly to Ren, embracing the entrancing feel of him. They were together, and everything would be fine now.

Chapter Sixteen
End of the Dorian Line

Ren had not taken them back to their mountainside manor, but to the Valder family home. As soon as they got there, however, there was a tense energy to the air, Meg's yellow magic floating around her.

"Something's wrong, Ren." Jinx said nervously.

His face immediately went neutral, nodding to her. He transported them to her library, Jinx having to hold back her gasp as the bookcases were empty of the books, some lit in a smoldering pile on the ground. The couch and chairs were toppled over, shredded as if by a wild animal. There was a dent in the metal stairs, easily the size of a grown person.

"Ren, we need to find your parents. I'll shield us." She urged.

She grabbed his hand, envisioning the sparkling blue of her magic over them. They left the library when she signaled they would be safe, moving through the winding halls of the manor.

Everything felt wrong to her, the magic hanging in the air like dust in sunlight. As they moved through it, the glitter swirled in circles. Everywhere they looked, the entire room was destroyed. Tables broken, windows cracked, things burning off to the sides. She had never seen such an array of destruction of a property without the building being demolished as well.

There was rustling and a frantic grunting as Jinx and Ren had turned to the eastern wing of the manor. The wing his parents resided in. Ren placed an arm before her, blocking her from whatever came their way.

A dark cape billowed behind a man dressed in a completely black spandex suit. A silver belt rested over his waist; fingerless gloves positioned over his hands where Jinx could see the black coloring of his fingers. A silver and black full-face mask was positioned over his head, two tear drop shaped eye holes allowing Jinx to see the black eyes of Knox.

"Dad-."

"They took her." He growled.

"Who took who?" Jinx asked, pushing Ren's arm away.

"Packard took Meg. He took my fucking wife." Knox snarled.

Jinx placed a hand to her mouth, holding in her gasp.

"What happened to you two?" He asked, pushing past them.

They turned following him down the hall towards the front door.

"We killed Micha and Thaddeus." Ren said.

"And we got married, but we'll worry about that later." Jinx added.

"Mazel tov." Knox grunted.

"Do you know where they even took her?" Ren asked.

Knox opened the large front doors to the mansion, Jinx never having seen them before looked at them with awe. One door was carved with a listing of Demented Doom's destruction, the other doing the same for the Cosmic Sorceress. Above the door, a stained-glass window held a black haired green eyed baby over the Valder family crest.

Outside, snow danced to the ground, their dark outfits bouncing off the white world around them. If Packard had taken Meg, the only place he would feel safe enough taking her would be the one place he took Jinx.

"They'd be at the torture cabin." Jinx said, both men turning to her. "It's surrounded by a field of red magic, I'm not sure where it comes from, but it's there, protecting them."

"And restricting us." Knox grumbled.

"I don't think so." Jinx pondered. "When they took me through it, it was almost like it was checking me over, not blocking me."

"An identification barrier?" Ren asked.

"Exactly." Jinx said.

Knox grumbled, looking out towards the distant Central City outline. "Can you take us there?"

Jinx nodded. "I can remember what it looks like, but only overhead."

Knox stepped forward, Ren putting himself between his father and Jinx. There was a growl within Ren's chest, one that even frightened her.

"Ren," Jinx soothed, moving around him and placing a hand on his arm. "We need to save your mom." She could see his jaw tighten as he hissed through his teeth.

"I promise I won't hurt her." Knox said to him.

Ren reluctantly stepped aside.

Knox looked to Jinx, placing one hand to her temple, the other to Ren's. "Ready?"

Jinx nodded, and the world around her shifted. She was flying over Honorville again, Thaddeus holding her in his arms. She looked below her, seeing the Dorian Estate, then passing over Lesser Honorville, where the small Heroes of Central City resided. Trees covered the ground, then, they passed through the red shield of light. A few moments later, a cabin with a rope hanging from a tree.

She gritted her teeth, and then the vision was gone and she was surrounded by white snow.

"Do you have it?" Knox asked darkly.

Ren nodded, pulling Jinx around the waist, and offering a hand to his father. "Let's go."

There was no snow on the ground as Ren, Knox, and Jinx arrived to the same tree where she had been whipped. The trough was still full of the muddied water, her blood stained on the ground just inches away. She scowled at the sight, her nose curling in disgust and anger.

There was a glowing to the cabin, an orange light from the fireplace inside. A cackling laugh sounded from inside, followed by a loud slap. Jinx could feel a difference in the air around her, not entirely sure what caused it.

"Be careful," She whispered, "Something is different."

The men nodded, Ren's little finger wrapping around hers.

They stepped towards the cabin, Knox kicking open the door. Inside, Meg was tied to a chair. Her curls had been crudely cut off in a pile on the floor around her, leaving her without the luscious halo Jinx had come to adore. Her right eye was swollen shut, a black and purple bruise already circling it. The sleeve of her dress was sliced open, crimson blood dried onto her pale skin.

She smiled menacingly as she saw the group, tilting her head to the side. "Hello darlings, I knew you would come."

Packard stood in front of the fireplace, his gloved navy-blue hands in fists beside him. His silver and blue suit did not look as it used to, his gut protruding outwards a bit, neck straining against the high collar. His hair was covered by a blue cap, lowering down to a mask that stopped above his nose.

"You look stupid." Jinx blurted in half a laugh.

Packard snarled, his teeth showing. "Traitor."

She shrugged. "You took my mother-in-law from me. I want her back."

Meg sucked in an excited gasp, smiling brightly. "You two got married?"

Ren nodded. "Killed Thaddeus and Micha while we were at it."

Jinx watched the color drain from Packard's face at the news, his snarling turning into a frown. "You killed my son?" He asked looking to Ren.

"No, she did." He looked to Jinx, with a snarky smile.

"Don't take it to heart, Packard, just doing what we Villains do best. Kill the people who wronged us." Jinx said casually.

Packard raced to her, Knox stepping between them, facing off in a battle that had lasted years. A battle Knox would not lose, fueled by the anger of Packard going after his weakness.

The door burst open, many of the police force surrounding the cabin, guns pinned on Ren and Jinx.

"Mind taking care of my mother?" He asked with a soft smile, taking a gun from the holster on her leg. "I'll get rid of these blue guys."

Jinx smiled kissing his cheek while ignoring the shouts from the same police commissioner who ordered her death. "Be careful now, I'll need you later."

"Yes ma'am." Ren smirked, saluting.

He vanished from inside, guns going off outside. Jinx smiled, then rushed to Meg.

"I am so excited for you, Jinx, you're such a good addition to the family." Meg gushed as if they were not in the middle of a dangerous situation.

"I'm happy too, but Ren wants to do a traditional wedding as well, so that will be in the future." Jinx giggled, struggling to untie the knots of the rope restraining Meg.

"There's a butter knife in that bag there. It's not ideal, but it's something." Meg grunted, displeased.

Jinx rushed to the bag, getting the polished silver butter knife from it. She paused, looking inside the bag when she saw women's clothing. Not just any woman's clothing, but Olivia's. She furrowed her brows, but went back to Meg, beginning to saw at the thick rope.

"I would love a grand baby soon," Meg began again, "Possibly a girl, so I can spoil her."

Jinx chuckled. "Meg, as much as I love the idea of children, it isn't on the top of my priorities right now."

"And what is?" She asked quizzically.

Jinx thought back to her personal goal of being able to bathe by herself. "Overcoming trauma, maybe."

Meg pursed her lips. "Yes, yes, that would be important before children." Jinx smiled, amused at the woman's focus on anything other than the fighting. "Of course, there is also the honeymoon phase you'll want to get over." Meg pondered, "Although, Knox and I never truly found there was an end to that."

"Honeymoon phase?" Jinx asked, a strand on the rope snapping.

"Oh yes, the constant intercourse everywhere is quite thrilling." She said, eyes clouding over with memories. "We practically destroyed every room with our enthusiasm."

Jinx paused. "Not my room, right?"

Meg looked to her, then laughed. "Honey, there wasn't the addition of your tower until Ren was sixteen and finally told us about you."

Jinx went back to sawing. "You built the tower for me?"

"Yes, why wouldn't we?" Meg giggled. "You were to be our future daughter-in-law, I'm honestly surprised it took Ren this long."

Jinx smiled, not realizing that she had been expected, not only by Ren, but his parents as well. Everything Ren had done for her, was encouraged by his parents.

"Did you know I was a Dorian?" Jinx asked.

Meg laughed. "That was the one thing he did keep from us, your name." The rope around her wrists broke free, Meg releasing her arms and rubbing them. "He didn't want me to come snooping, which I would have."

Jinx crouched down, beginning at her feet. "Meg, why can't you cast any spells to free yourself. I saw your magic all over the manor, but none here."

Meg's smile faded, turning into a deep angry frown. "Olivia Dorian."

Jinx frowned. "What about her?"

"The reason the Dorian family is so prominent in society is because of your-I mean-Olivia." Meg said, "She is not just another Love Interest, she was powerful too. Could have been a Hero, but was placed as a Love Interest, which surprised everyone in her sorting."

"What do you mean?" Jinx asked.

"Olivia Dorian was in my class growing up, she was not popular, not all that pretty either. She came from a BC family who were poor, broken, and so no one expected anything from her." Meg paused. "In her sorting, she was named a Love Interest, and the next day, a burst of power shook Central City. I couldn't use my magic, no one could."

"She was powerful enough to limit the entirety of Central City's Villains and Heroes on accident, so she became a target, naturally." Meg stopped, hesitating, like she was thinking of the proper words. "Olivia was married to Packard, had Thaddeus, and then when out on a walk with other Hero's wives, was kidnapped."

Jinx furrowed her brows, knife snapping a strand of the rope. "Olivia was kidnapped by Elias Ursu, the last known member of the Ursu family." She smiled down to Jinx lovingly. "When Olivia returned, Elias was dead, and she was pregnant, the baby coming out with brown hair and gray eyes, just like Elias."

Jinx's mouth dropped open, pausing. "Are you saying I'm a product of rape?"

"Oh gosh no darling. Olivia was Elias' weakness, there was nothing not consensual about their relationship. In fact, from what I saw of them while Knox courted me, they looked happy."

"Then why did he die?" Jinx asked.

"That is a mystery I have yet to solve."

Jinx saw Knox crash through a window, Packard flying through after him.

"I loved him." Olivia's voice said from behind Jinx.

Jinx slowly turned, placing the knife in Meg's lap. Olivia pointed a revolver to Jinx, the gun pointed to her chest. "Then why did he die?"

Olivia shook her head, tears in her eyes. "Because I was a Love Interest. I was Packard's Love Interest. Society saw me as powerful and good, the only thing I wanted. Attention, beauty, power. Do you know what they would've seen me as if I had abandoned my child and husband? The same as if I was a Background Character. Nothing."

"So I am your child," Jinx said softly, praying for the good side of her mother to see what she was doing, killing off her own blood. "But I am not a Dorian."

Olivia nodded, her chin wobbling. "I prayed you would come out like me, so Packard wouldn't suspect, but you came out like Elias."

"The beatings-."

"Because you were an Ursu and a constant reminder of my adultery." Olivia shook.

Tears welled up in Jinx's eyes, her body stiffening. "How could you let him do that to me? Then to cover it up?"

"Because I was a Dorian!" She screamed, "You were a Dorian as far as anyone knew, your hair and eyes coming from a long lost relative of mine. We had an appearance to keep up!"

Jinx shook her head. "You were my mother, my only protection against him! How could you abandon me?"

Olivia's face contorted into an expression of disgust. "I gave you everything. Food, a roof over your head, lessons in self defense. You were given everything I never was."

"You forgot about abuse, solitary confinement, the idea that I would have to hide who I really was to be liked." Jinx scoffed walking towards her. "You let Thaddeus go on that quest to change my sorting. You knew what could have happened if I was re-sorted."

Olivia raised her chin. "I did what I had to do to keep our family name prominent in society."

There was a gunshot.

Jinx looked down, the barrel of the revolver smoking, pressed against her stomach. She looked back up to Olivia, who pulled back the hammer again, only to be thrown to the ground by Meg. Jinx watched as Meg quickly took the gun, pointed it at Olivia's head and fired. Officially leaving Jinx an orphan.

Meg's worried face came into view as Jinx placed a hand to the wound, raising it to her face to see her blood coating it. Obviously, the corset body armor would not stop a bullet being fired that close to her.

"I fucked up." Jinx said softly, her knees giving out as Meg held her.

"No, no, darling, you did everything right." Meg whispered, brushing back the loose strands of her hair.

"Ren." Jinx coughed, holding pressure to the wound.

Meg screamed for him, Ren appearing within seconds.

His face went pale, mouth slacking open, his eyebrows pushed upwards. Ren fell to the floor beside her, his entire body shaking as he took her in his arms.

"Pressure on the wound." Jinx gasped, the pain finally hitting her. "Hospital, fourth floor, surgical ward. It's too far to the right."

He nodded, looking to his mother. There was a crackling aura of yellow energy that encompassed her, eyes turning yellow, stars flying around her.

Jinx blinked, Ren now carrying her into the hospital. "I need a doctor!" He screamed. "If you don't save her I'm going to kill everyone!"

Doctors rushed to her, placing her on a hospital bed. They tore at her clothes, getting a better look at the gunshot wound.

"Get her to surgery now!" One doctor ordered, the bed moving quickly down the hall.

"Ren." Jinx whispered, forcing her eyes from closing.

She couldn't see him, only heard him yelling her name. Her head lolled to the side, and everything went dark.

Born in the winter on the Dorian Estate, after thirteen hours of intensive labor, Jinx Ursu, last of the Ursu family line, was born. Her name meaning bad luck, she had no father, and a resentful mother. Taken care of by simple Background Characters, it was the only reason Jinx had survived.

After years of abuse and kept in the dark, Jinx Ursu was sorted as a Background Character, much to her family's displeasure. Though, deep down, her mother was grateful. That was, until she was re-sorted as Morally Gray, neither good nor bad, but no place in society.

After several months of torture, love, and sacrifice, Jinx Ursu had abandoned the name she had been given from the Dorian family, embracing the one she had chosen for herself, Valder.

Jinx opened her eyes, the lights of the hospital room bright. She went to sit up, pain radiating through her body, causing her to lean back.

"Take it easy, Valder." Ren smiled to her softly.

"Fuck that hurt." She moaned.

Ren chuckled, running a hand over her hair. "I bet it did, you just went through a seven-hour surgery to stop your liver from bleeding, then to find the bullet inside you."

"I could've done it in six." She smiled weakly.

Ren laughed, kissing her forehead. "I'm sure you could've."

Jinx furrowed her brows as she thought back to everything that happened. Fear built inside her, knowing they had left Knox and Meg behind.

"Mom and dad are safe," Ren said, "Packard and most of the police force dead, or severely injured."

"Did he suffer?" Jinx asked darkly.

"It's funny, mom had the most brilliant idea to string him up by his wrists to a tree, my father whipping him until he almost bled out. Then, my mother would heal him, beginning the process all over again." Ren smirked.

Jinx sighed, glad to be finally over with the entire situation. "I am so ready to go home and do nothing, I don't care how boring it gets."

Ren laughed. "That's good, since I don't plan on paying for the medical expenses."

Jinx laughed, it turning to a groan, holding her side.

"I know I'm funny Valder, but please try not to harm yourself."

Jinx shook her head. "Not Valder, Ursu. You're Valder, but my real name is Jinx Ursu."

Ren smiled. "Is that what you would prefer? Jinx Ursu?"

Jinx nodded. "Though I do not think I attract the bad luck as my name suggests."

"That you are not." Ren said, removing the cords from her body gently. "Now, let's get you home."

She cringed as he lifted her from the bed, her arms wrapping around his neck. She felt the cool breeze behind her, realizing she was not clothed in anything but a hospital gown.

"Did they ruin my Villain suit?" She pouted.

"Unfortunately, yes."

Her hand then went to her neck, the necklace gone, as was her ring.

"I have them at home, don't worry."

She sighed, resting into him. "I would've cried."

He kissed her head, moments later setting her down in the silken gray sheets of their bed. "I can't have you crying, Ursu."

She crinkled her nose. "Even that name sounds wrong."

"I wasn't going to say anything, but it does." He laughed.

"Whatever, just lay beside me." She said, flipping the covers over on the other side of the bed. "I don't think we've actually slept in this bed a full night."

Ren slid under the covers beside her, kissing the side of her face as he brushed back her hair. "We were a bit preoccupied."

She smiled as his arm slid under her and she leaned into his chest. "This is home."

Ren hummed his agreement.

"Can we get that healer to come? I would like to get healed faster than normal." She smirked.

"Ulterior motives, my dear?" Ren chuckled.

She rolled to face him. "Mr. Valder, you should know exactly what my motives are, I am your weakness after all."

Ren practically ran out of bed at her words, causing her to smile.

"I'm going to call the healer." He shouted.

Jinx sighed into her pillow. It smelled like lemon balm and lavender, allowing her to close her eyes. What a beautiful life she created from the traumas of her past. A world where Heroes and Villains lived, and magic flowed through her veins. A world where she could see a small boy with black hair running around their property between the hidden mountains, one eye gray and another eye green. Her world.

Epilogue

After years of living in her mountain side home, Jinx was still amazed at the collection of flowers that bloomed every spring right alongside the river.

She sat on the blanket she had made, finding herself quite an expert quilter after she had finished writing her book on *venenum flos*. A basket of fruits, cheeses, and a pitcher of lemonade sat beside her as she looked out over the scenery before her.

"Mama, Nisha took my doll and put it in the pocket realm." Zilla complained.

"She is *my* doll, I can do what I want with her." Nisha objected.

Jinx looked over her daughters with raised eyebrows. Her oldest, Nisha, was just as Ren had wanted. Black hair, gray eyes, and a smirk that surpassed the sass in Ren's. Zilla, on the other hand, was a copy of herself. Brown wavy hair, gray eyes, and a soft smile that came from her shy side.

"Nisha, we talked about putting toys in the pocket realm, give it back." Jinx scolded, though deep down she was proud of Nisha.

She had been three when Meg had excitedly come to Jinx with the news that Nisha was magically inclined. Nisha had shown how she opened a tear into the fabric of their world, a dark place that seemed to come from nowhere. It had scared her at first, worried her baby girl would fall into it and never return. Nisha, did not fall into it, using it as a portal to go from one place to another, and to hide toys from her siblings.

Nisha reluctantly opened up the pocket realm, retrieving a doll with braided hair, a sewn on face of another doll, all extremities mix matched from other dolls, and a simple pink dress.

Zilla snatched the doll from Nisha, patting down her hair. "Thank you very much." She sassed, going back to the edge of the river.

Nisha huffed, walking into the pocket realm and appearing farther down the river, throwing rocks into the water.

"Another fight?" Ren asked.

Jinx looked back to him, smiling as she reached up. He grinned, giving her their baby boy, only a year old. He cooed happily, black hair already covering most of his head, his eyes, pure green.

Ren sat beside her, plucking a wilted flower, placing it in her hair. "Elias, here, was not too happy about being changed."

"Oh?" Jinx asked amused.

"It was quite interesting. He levitated the diaper across the room." Ren smirked proudly.

"Isn't it strange how they aren't even in school yet and their powers manifested?" Jinx asked.

Ren shook his head, playing with a loose strand of her hair. "I got my power at seven, my mother got hers when she was an infant, my father when he hit puberty."

"I wonder what Zilla will get." Jinx pondered, looking as her daughter dismantled the doll she had retrieved back from Nisha.

Ren laughed. "A sense of dismantling people. Should we be scared?"

Jinx giggled. "Not yet, but a surgical kit for her birthday might be a good idea."

Ren raised his eyebrows, looking to her. "You're encouraging this?"

"Why wouldn't I?" Jinx smirked. "She is our daughter, exploring a career in healthcare."

Ren shook his head. "God, do I love you."

He leaned over, Jinx accepting his kiss. "You better."

"Nisha, Zilla, come get something to eat." Ren called over, causing Zilla to run, and Nisha to portal to them.

Jinx's family sat around her, all beautiful and gifted, destined to be great Heroes or Villains, she didn't care. As long as they were happy, that's all that mattered.

"Zilla, you start school soon, do you know what you want to be sorted as?" Ren asked, smiling.

Zilla put a finger to her chin, a smirk forming on her small face. "I want to be like mama," She announced, "Morally Gray."

More by

Anna Lynn Hammar

The Cursed Fates Series

The Shield of Hope

The Blade of Truth

The Ring of Promise